The Magdalen Martyrs

Ken Bruen

The Magdalen Martyrs

ST. MARTIN'S MINOTAUR NEW YORK

www.minotaurbooks.com

ISBN 0-312-31645-3
EAN 978-0312-31645-7

First published in Ireland by Brandon, an imprint of Mount Eagle Publications

First U.S. Edition: March 2005

10 9 8 7 6 5 4 3 2 1

To Jason Starr, Craig McDonald, and Charlie Stella, stars ascending

The Magdalen Martyrs

PROLOGUE

The girl was on her knees, polishing the floor. She was dressed in shapeless faded overalls. A spotless white apron bore witness to the laundry she was confined to. For three hours she'd been attempting to bring a high gloss to the floor. She knew it wouldn't be complete till the very surface reflected her face. The baby she'd had to give up hung like a wound on her soul, searing the very prayers she was trying to mouth.

A dizzy spasm hit her and she bent forward, mopped her brow with a rag from beneath her sleeve. She heard footsteps and the click of heels on the wooden floor, a nun approaching. The voice came like a lash.

"Who told you to stop working, you lazy trollop?"

She knew better than to answer back but did lift her head momentarily to see which of the nuns it was. The swish of the heavy black beads came too quickly for her to duck, and it caught her full across the face, cutting her cheek and laying a welt along the ridge of her eye. The blood came spurting, marking the clean floor. The nun raised the beads again, saying,

"Now look at the state of that floor, you heathen street-walker."

The girl bit her lower lip as she fought not to cry out. If they saw you weep, it seemed to incite them to even worse excesses. In her mind she called to a God who had so long ago deserted her, and there was no family she could ever appeal to. The nun was already raising the beads for a third and lethal blow.

December is a rough month. Screw all that festive preparation. If you're on your own, it mocks you at every turn. You open an old book and find a list of friends you once sent cards to. Now, they're all dead or disappeared. The television is crammed with toys for children you never had, and boy, is it ever too late. The radio is playing ballads that once held significance or even hope.

It has been said that you truly only realise the full impact of being alone when you're in the kitchen, as you prepare a meal for one. Everything is singular: one cup, one set of cutlery, one plate and, probably, one lousy plan. Live long enough alone and you develop obsessive traits. As soon as the meal is done, you wash the plate. Why? Who the hell is going to complain? Let the shit stack up for a week and see who cares; but you don't because you can't. The rituals you have developed are all that tie you to the human race, and the worst bit is the knowledge you are doing this.

Man, I'd gone through some different homes these past years. I'd had a flat along the canal, and if not happy there, I was as near to content as it gets. Got evicted and moved to Bailey's

Hotel, one of the few remaining private ones in Galway.

Then, as the result of a case I was investigating, I seemed to land on my uppers and moved to a house in Hidden Valley. That was fine. Had me a time. Stone floors, open fireplace, deep freeze, neighbours, books . . . in a wooden bookcase . . . the whole citizen deal. But blew that to hell and gone with the worst judgement call of my chequered career. I feel the guilt and recriminations still. The line of dead who accuse me at every turn of sleep, they come in silent dread, the eyes fixed on me as I twist and moan in vain hope of escape.

So I drink. I'm way past my sell-by date and am on precious borrowed time. I should have gone down a long time ago. Lots of days, I wish I had.

The first two weeks of December I was dry. Gearing up. I knew I'd never get through the whole fiasco sober so was putting in time for good behaviour. It's just another delusion that alcoholics practise. These lies are nearly as vital as the alcohol. You hug them close as prayer, and they are twice as heartfelt. The constant rain and the fecking cold, it permeates your bones. Along the way, I'd been seriously addicted to cocaine but was even refraining from that. So, I had the chills and shakes and, of course, a major dose of them blues.

I was living again in Bailey's Hotel. Located near the tourist office, it is not easy to find and survives against the odds. Owned by a widow in her eighties, for some reason she has affection for me and continues to keep a room for me despite my worst excesses. She is under the impression I helped her out once; and if I did, I've forgotten how or even when. I'm grateful she doesn't judge me. Perhaps it's that we are both of that endangered species, "Old Galway", and our time is truly limited. When we go, the hotel will be converted to luxury apartments, and some yuppy will tread on the bones of our deluded selves.

Her staff consists mainly of Janet, a woman as old as herself, who is pot-walloper, maid, conscience, cleaner and as religious a woman as I've ever met. Because I read so many books, Janet thinks I'm somebody. This is an old Irish notion that, alas, fools fewer and fewer people. I had a calendar on the wall. The Sacred Heart was on the front, and the days were marked with pithy sayings to uplift your day. I can't say they much uplifted mine. In red, the 18th stood out like a beacon. It's my father's birthday. That was the day I'd drink again. Just knowing the very time when I'd lift a glass got me through so many other impossible hours. I'd planned well. Had four bottles of black Bushmill's, twenty-four pint cans of Guinness and an ounce of coke. I kid you not, this was just for openers; and for the lock-down days of Christmas, I thought it was a fairly decent plan.

The day came and I lashed in with a vengeance. Managed a week till I got a blackout and ended back in hospital. They were not pleased to see me and read me a minor riot act. Their hearts weren't in it, as they knew I'd drink again. Mid-January, I was back in Bailey's, trying to ration my drinking, abstaining from coke and suffering a depression like the depths of hell. Sitting on the edge of my bed, I was running some lines of Ann Kennedy in my head.

Burial Instructions

These lines:

> *You might know the spot*
> *Because that's where they placed*
> *Marilyn's ashes*

In a pale marble crypt
Looking across at our family.

Go figure.
I can't.

There's a pub in Balham that's exclusively for the insane. About a hundred yards from the bingo hall, which is appropriate. Even the staff are seriously deranged. When I was hurting, which was often, I'd go there and blend. You always met someone who knew hell from the inside. Shortly after my marriage, I'd gone there, ordered a pint and a whiskey, considered my future. A guy next to me was dropping soluble aspirin into a pint of mild.

I didn't ask.

He said,

"You're dying to ask."

Took a look at him. A tattoo on his neck that was either an anchor or a swastika, a scar that ran from his left eyebrow to his upper lip. As often is, he had gentle eyes. Sure, there was lunacy, but you can't preserve that gentleness with sanity. I said,

"If you want to tell me."

Nice neutral territory. He savoured my answer, then,

"Stops the hangover."

"Right."

Then, oh so very carefully, he slid the glass to his left and shouted up a pint of bitter. He said,

"The trick is not to drink it."

For that day and precious few others, I was wearing the wedding band. Bright and glowing, in that place it reeked of another country. He fastened on the glow, said,

"You're married."

"Yeah."

"You know the best thing 'bout that."

"No."

"They can't call you queer."

I had recently got my customary letter from

THE DEPARTMENT OF JUSTICE

A Chara,

It has come to our notice that you have failed to return an item of equipment.

We draw your attention to Article 59347A of Uniform and Equipment on page 25 of the manual. Said Item No. 8234, a garda all-weather coat, remains the property of the Department.

We anticipate the speedy return of said item.

Mise le meas,

B. Cosgrove

I did what I always did.

Crumpled it and lobbed it fast across the room. I'd been receiving variations of the same letter for years. No matter where I lived, by the canal, in Bailey's Hotel, London or Hidden Valley, these missives eventually found me.

I'd been a guard, and if not the finest years of my life, they were certainly the ones that made the most sense. I'd trained at Templemore and had the makings of a fine career.

It seems odd now but I truly cared then. The first time I walked down the street in my uniform with the buttons gleaming, my cap at a firm angle, the baton to hand, I thought I could make a difference. The first wake-up call came about a month into my duty. I was on night patrol, an older sergeant walking point. We got a call to a domestic and arrived to find a drunken husband locked outside his house. The sergeant said,

"If we have to arrest him, stand to his rear."

I thought he doubted my courage, and sure enough, after we tried to talk to the man, he became abusive and we cautioned him. He told us to go fuck ourselves, and the sergeant said to arrest him, winking at me. Full of youth and bravado, I went face to face with the guy, and he vomited all over me. I can still hear the sergeant laughing. The next few years were good till I grew overfond of the jar and it became a cause of concern to my superiors, and I was eventually slung out. I kept the all-weather coat, and it was a reminder of the one chance of meaning I could have given my life.

That garment was my sole link to my career. If not validation, at least it was proof.

My previous case had provided accommodation, a house in Hidden Valley. To coin a London phrase, I'd been living it large. It ended in disaster. I'd moved back to Bailey's Hotel.

Mrs Bailey, you felt she'd known the signatories of 1916. She had that fresh flawless skin almost patented by nuns. Her eyes were a blend of wisdom and mischief. Can there be a better combination? Once, she'd told me,

"There'll always be a room for you here."

Now that may not count as wealth, but it's a richness of rare elevation. A retired judge had taken my old room. He was old Galway, too, so that's all the reference he needed. I was given the attic. I liked it. The skylight gave a false sense of light. All the essentials:

> Shower
>
> Kettle
>
> Phone
>
> TV.

Didn't take me long to unpack. Yet again, I was down to the basics:

> Age Concern suit
>
> Leather jacket
>
> Item 8234
>
> Three jeans
>
> Bally boots
>
> Sneakers.

And, of course, my books.

Music too. All of

> Johnny Duhan
>
> the Cowboy Junkies
>
> John Stewart
>
> Van Morrison.

"I built a house and found—why was I surprised?—Thoreau was right.
If a man builds a barn, the barn becomes a prison."

Gary Paulsen, *Pilgrimage on a Steel Ride*

A Monday morning, late January, I had an alcoholic fit. Doesn't
get more serious than that. Put me smack back in hospital.
A doctor looming over me said,

"Mr Taylor, have you any idea what happened to you?"

"No."

"The next attack could kill you."

"I'll be careful."

He looked down at my chart, shook his head, said,

"Care isn't what's needed. You cannot drink."

The episode terrorised me. When I got out of the hospital,
I didn't drink. But I'd been down that road a thousand times.
Sooner or later, the edge of the fear dropped off or I got to
"Who gives a fuck?" and drank.

I sank into deep and deeper depression. Getting out of bed
became increasingly difficult. During the night, massive anxiety
would pull me from sleep, on the hour, every hour. Drained, I'd
crawl from bed and have to force myself to the shower. Food
held no interest, but I tried. Asked myself, "Why bother?"
Shaved my beard and was horrified at how sunken my face was.
But hell, I'd great teeth.

In my last case, two brothers had come after me. If they lived in America, they'd have been trailer trash. Here, they were "bachelors". Implying, it was their choice. Among their agenda of hatred were tinkers. I'd been working for the travellers. Coming home from a funeral, I'd been pissed and eating chips, the Irish Nirvana or, as purists might say, *"Tír na nÓg"*.

The brothers had hit me in the mouth with an iron bar. Weeks of dentistry resulted in a smile that glowed.

I'd once heard depression described as being under murky, fetid water and not being able to break the surface.

That fit.

Each day was drearier than the one before. The high point was going to bed so I'd be able to just cease. If comfort could be squeezed from anything, it was the thought of suicide. It is deep shit when that's the only light. Months before, I'd been drinking in a dive off Merchant's Road. What drew me was the menace, palpable in the very air. A Russian sailor, dry-docked for eight months, sold me a .32-calibre Heckler & Koch. It's a nasty piece of work; I was amazed to get it, and so cheap.

Most nights, I'd hold it in my hand and think,

"One movement up, then squeeze the trigger."

I cannot say why I didn't. Tried to return to books. There had always been reading. No matter what went down, I could always read. Wasn't working any more. All my old reliable ones,

> Thomas Merton
> Nelson Algren
> Walter Macken
> Francis Thompson.

Nope.

Weren't doing it.

Returned to a writer who'd give me the blackness. Derek Raymond, the founder of English noir. Also known as Robin

Cook. He had a lifelong affinity with the criminal, the dam-
aged. Educated at that "hotbed of buggery", Eton, it was, he
said, "an excellent preparation for vice of any kind". Prompted
by an almost terminal boredom, he absconded, first to Paris
and the legendary Beat Hotel, then New York's Lower East
Side. The first of his five marriages went down the toilet after
sixty-five days.

My own marriage had run almost parallel. I didn't plan on
four more.

He said,

*I knew things were going wrong when I got home, put the shop-
ping down in the kitchen and the table gave a terrible cough.*

No wonder I loved him.

He wrote a spate of books that drew a cult following. Translated as good reviews, no money. It didn't worry him unduly.
He said,

*I've watched people like Kingsley Amis, struggling to get on
the up escalator, while I had the down escalator all to myself.*

Here's when I like him best.

Nearing fifty, he began the Factory novels. Unremittingly
black thrillers, the protagonist haunted by personal tragedy and
obsessed with the deaths no one else bothers with, they show
London in despair. Scoured by "vile psychic weather".

The books culminated in the astonishing *I Was Dora Suarez*,
He wrote of his novel *In Mourning,*

*If I had no guilt to purge, I would not have known where the road
to hell was, . . . she was my atonement for 50 years indifference*

to the miserable state of this world, a terrible journey through my
own guilt, and the guilt of others.

Liver cancer and booze took him out of the game at the age
of sixty-three. I'd lined up his works by the wall, like a series
of bullets I had to simply load. His final years, he lived in a
Spartan bedsit in Willesden.

If I hadn't known to mourn him back then, I was making
up for that now.

I could feel his finger on the trigger of my Heckler & Koch.

In my previous case, I'd enlisted the help of a hard man
named Bill Cassell. I asked him to protect a young girl and he
did so. Then I further indebted myself by asking him to elimi-
nate a killer. Such help doesn't come cheap. Gave him a shitpile
of money, but it was the favour he'd call in one day that was
most worrying. You owe a man like him, you have to deliver,
and the dread is waiting to see what it is he will ask. At the time,
he does warn you, but I went ahead and made the trade. He is
your seriously hard man; even the guards give him a wide berth.
He doesn't have perimeters, there is no line he won't cross, and
you better hope you are not the one he is crossing that line to
see. The call came on a Sunday night. He opened with,

"You're a hard man to find."

"You managed."

Low chuckle.

"Yeah."

"How is your health, Bill?"

With liver cancer, how could it be? But I felt I should at least
make an effort. He said,

"Fucked,"

"I'm sorry, Bill."

"You'll know why I'm calling, Jack."

"My chit's due?"

"Right."

"What do you want?"

"Not on the phone. Sweeney's at twelve, tomorrow."

"I'm off the booze."

"I heard. You won't be there long."

"I suppose that's a comfort."

"Take it where you find it."

"I'll try."

"Twelve, Jack, don't be late."

Click.

The depression sat on me like cement. I knew Bill's call had to come, but now I couldn't even rise to anxiety. All dealings with Bill required a high level of unease. Forced myself to put on my coat, get out for a walk. What I wanted was to curl up in a corner and weep. As I passed reception, Mrs Bailey said,

"Mr Taylor!"

"Jack, please."

I knew she'd never get that familiar. Her face was concerned. She asked,

"Are you all right?"

"Touch of flu."

We let that float above our heads for a moment. Then she said,

"You could do with a tonic."

"Right."

She looked like she'd a ton to add but let it slide, said,

"If there's anything I can do . . ."

"Thanks."

I walked to Eyre Square.

Gangs of young people milling about, all with cans of lager, flasks of cider.

    Booze

    Booze

    Booze

I went to Nestor's. Jeff was tending bar. He was the picture of
health. He and his girlfriend Cathy had recently had a baby,
a Down's syndrome baby. He said,

"Jeez, Jack, where have you been?"

"Low profile."

"Are you doing OK? You look, I dunno, kind of haunted."

I juggled that expression, repeated,

"Haunted, now there's a term. I'm off cigs, coke and booze.
Why on earth would I be less than par?"

He was astonished, said,

"Even the cigs . . . the coke . . . Christ, Jack, I'm impressed."

The sentry, in a semi-stupor since Christmas, raised his head,
said,

"Good on yah,"

and slumped back on the counter.

In the days I drank in Grogan's, there were always two men
propping up the bar, one at each end, dressed in identical donkey jackets, cloth caps, Terylene pants. Sentries, I called them.
They never spoke to each other. No acknowledgement ever.
In front of them, always a half drained pint; no matter what

hour you came upon them, the level of the glass never varied. When Grogan's changed hands, one had a heart attack and the other moved to Nestor's. Jeff said,

"There was a young guy, looking for you."

"How young?"

"Twenty-five maybe."

"That's young. What did he want?"

"Something about work."

"Did he give a name?"

He rooted through a pile of papers, found it, read,

"Terry Boyle."

"What did you make of him?"

"Um . . . polite. Oh yeah, he had a good suit."

"And that tells us what?"

"I don't know. If he comes in again, you want me to ask him anything?"

"Yeah, ask him where he got the suit."

I went back to the hotel, muttering,

"See, was that so difficult? You were in a pub, didn't drink, you did good."

As I lay on my bed, I asked myself,

"Did that make you feel better?"

Did it fuck?

I'd read Alvarez's study of suicide, The Savage God. *Got to the* chapter where he discussed his own failed attempt.

Whatever else, I didn't want to screw it up. Read what the medical experts had to say.

This.

Most suicides will communicate their intentions, verbally or non verbally.

I reached for a cigarette, realised I wasn't smoking any more. Continued.

In America, they have QPR intervention: questioning, persuading, referring. I was reading about it in the paper.

How it worked was you listened, then talked the PS, the potential suicide, into getting professional help, fast. The hot phase of a suicide crisis was three weeks. Potential suicides make predictions, like "I'll be dead before Christmas" or "I'll never see the summer."

I then waded through a mess of medical terminology, until I came to

Gatekeepers are the first people to realise the potential suicide is serious. They are the first "finder". It's their duty, responsibility, to direct the potential suicide towards help.

I stopped reading. So at last I could call myself something. A "PS", ending up like an afterthought to a letter.

Gatekeepers! The pity was I hadn't anyone to fill the role.

Sweeney's is a hard pub. Anyone who strays in there is quickly shown the door.

Welcome is not part of the deal. Bill Cassell had held court there for as long as I remember. When I walked in, the place went quiet. Then, as it registered who I was, conversations resumed. I was at least familiar. Bill was at his usual table, looking even worse than before. The eyes, though, they were as bright and unyielding as ever. He said,

"I ordered coffee."

"Coffee's good."

I took the seat opposite him. The barman brought the coffee. No one spoke. When he'd gone, Bill said,

"You don't look so good, Jack."

"Clean living is killing me."

"You owe me double, Jack."

"Right."

"Well, I'm going to let you clean the sheet with one job."

"OK."

He sat back, fixed his eyes on me, asked,

"What do you know about the Magdalen laundry?"

"The Maggies?"

Anger lit his eyes, and he snapped,

"Don't call them that."

The Magdalen girls were called thus. In the fifties, unwed mothers were placed there by their families or the Church. Conditions were appalling and the girls subjected to horrendous abuse. Only recently had the full story been revealed.

He asked,

"Do you remember my mother?"

"No . . ."

"She was there. Had a terrible time. They shaved her head, wrapped her in wet sheets. But she escaped, met my father, and they had me. I learnt most of this from my father, after her death. There was a woman there, named Rita Monroe. It was she who helped my mother escape."

He stopped. The story seemed to have drained him. I waited till he regained some energy, asked,

"What is it you want me to do?"

"Find Rita Monroe."

"Can't you do that yourself?"

"I've tried."

"But after all this time, she's probably dead."

"So be it. If she is alive, I'd like to thank her in person."

"Jeez, Bill, it's a reach. Was she a nun?"

"No, one of the lay staff they sometimes employed. You have a knack of finding resolutions; somehow or other, you get the job done."

"I'll give it a try."

"Give it better than that, Jack. You may or may not know I have some new help, apart from my usual boy. That's the big one who wears a white tracksuit. He's the one you see, but my new boy, now him you don't want to see, not ever. He's from Dublin, and I use him to . . . let's say . . . terminate a debt. Trust me, but you don't ever want to see him. You'll smell him first, because the crazy fuck, he's always chewing Juicy Fruit, the gum? He comes up behind you, and you think you've been ambushed by an air freshener. I tell you . . . Nev, he's a tonic."

I didn't reply; my eyes strayed to the bar, the spirit bottles calling me. He said,

"And stay sober."

I figured we were done, got up to leave, when he said,

"No doubt you'll have heard the stories about me."

The stories were legion. Usually involving ferocious retribution. I nodded and he said,

"The fast food place, they got that wrong."

One of the most repeated. The owner owed Bill money and wasn't paying up. The yarn went that Bill had pushed the guy's face into the fat fryer. He said,

"I didn't put his face in the fat."

"I never believed it anyway."

He looked straight at me, said,

"It was his balls."

After leaving Bill, I felt a lightening of my spirit. Not a whole lot but enough for me to answer someone who shouted hello. It was the first break in the darkness for so long. I didn't expect to find Rita Monroe, but at least I could make the effort.

Back at the hotel, I began. Asked Mrs Bailey,

"Did you ever hear of a Monroe?"

"From Galway?"

"I don't know . . . a Rita Monroe."

She gave it serious thought, then,

"No, it's an unusual name so I'd remember. Ask Janet. She knows everyone."

Janet didn't know either. Next, to the phone directory, found ten Monroes listed. Rang them all. No Rita in any of them or even relatives. Went to the parish records and drew another blank. Course, she could be married. What I needed was someone familiar with the Magdalen. Walked down to Forster Street to where it had been located.

Demolished now, luxury apartments on the site. I wondered if the new occupiers were aware of what had been here. An elderly man was coming down the hill, measuring his steps with extreme care. He caught my eye, said,

"Howyah."

I figured it was an outside shot, said,

"Howyah yourself. You're a Galwegian, I'd say."

"Born and bred."

This, with a mixture of pride. I asked,

"Do you remember the Magdalen?"

He gave me an irritated look, as if I'd questioned his faculties. Near shouted,

"And why wouldn't I?"

"No, I didn't mean any offence. It's just you don't hear much about it."

He spat on the road, said,

"Best forgotten. It was like a concentration camp. They were worse than the Nazis."

"Who?"

"Anyone involved in the running of it. May they roast in hell."

He brushed past me, his piece spoken. I went to Nestor's. The sentry was in place, with the habitual half pint. Jeff was stocking up, said,

"Jack, you look better."

"I feel it."

"What'll I get you, coffee?"

"Sure. Could I have a word with Cathy?"

"Yeah."

He shouted for her, then turned back to me, asked,

"You working on something?"

"Maybe."

"You have that gleam in your eye. Not that you'd listen, but is it a good idea? The last couple of cases nearly killed you."

"This is different."

"I hope so, I really do."

Cathy came down and, first off, a huge hug. She said,

"You shaved the beard."

"What can I tell you? A change if not an improvement."

She examined me, said,

"You could do with some nourishment."

I listened to her voice with amazement. Cathy was a hard edged London punk when I met her. She had tracks on her arms and a mouth as foul as the weather. Then she'd met Jeff and gone native. Traces of London still lingered in her expressions, but they were becoming scarce. I missed the old version. She said,

"Your eyes and skin are clear."

"So?"

"So you've kicked."

"I'm trying."

"There is help, AA, NA."

I shook my head and she said,

"It's nearly impossible to do it alone."

"Can we move on to something else? I need your help."

In the past, Cathy had proved very resourceful. She had a knack of not only tracking down information but doing it quickly. She asked,

"What do you need?"

"Ever hear of the Magdalen?"

"No."

"OK, I'm trying to trace a woman named Rita Monroe."

"No problem, I'll get right on it."

She didn't ask anything further, so I said,

"I'll pay you, of course."

"That would be a first."

Brendan Flood was an ex-garda who'd discovered religion. My first encounter, he'd half killed me, broken my fingers and left me for dead. By a strange set of circumstances, we'd become unlikely allies. He'd helped me solve a case. The last time I'd enlisted his help, I ignored his contribution and an innocent man was killed. I hadn't seen him since.

Rang him and, reluctantly, he agreed to meet. As usual, he chose Supermacs. There he'd look longingly at large containers of curried chips. I'd offer to buy, he'd decline, as penance. I got there first, got a double cheeseburger and a milkshake. Was picking at these when he arrived. He was wearing a donkey jacket, leather patches on the sleeves. It was open to reveal a heavy silver cross on an even heavier chain. I said,

"Thanks for meeting me."

"It was God's will."

I pushed the food aside and he said,

"It is sinful to waste that."

"You want it?"

"I'm abstaining."

"Naturally."

He sat, folded his hands like a supplicant or an ejit, said,

"I believe you've turned over a new leaf."

"You what?"

"That you've abandoned your various vices."

"More like them abandoning me."

He gave a small smile, piety leaking from the corners, said,

"Our prayers were answered."

"What?"

"Our Tuesday night group; we prayed for you by name."

"Thanks."

He leaned over, put a hand on my arm, said,

"Now you've begun on the path, you should come and bear witness. People speak in tongues."

"Yeah, any of them civil?"

He withdrew his hand as if burned, said,

"Be careful of mockery, Jack Taylor."

I was getting a headache, asked,

"Could you check on somebody for me?"

He shook his head, said,

"Dire consequences tend to accompany you."

"Look, this is a different deal. There was a woman, Rita Monroe, who was a decent human being."

He thought it over, asked,

"You wish to locate this woman?"

"That's it."

"I shall meditate and ask the Lord for direction."

Buoyed by my activities, I got a takeaway curry, settled in front
of the TV. Watched for a few hours without registering a whole
lot. Then *Buffy* came on. Despite myself, I started to pay attention. Count Dracula had a guest appearance. Buffy asked him
why he'd come. He hissed,

"For the sun?"

Was smiling despite myself. *Angel* followed next. He's a vam-
pire good guy. This episode, he was forced to sing in a demon
karaoke bar, despite protesting,

"Three things I don't do: tan, date and sing in public."

He mangled Barry Manilow's "Mandy". But the MC, who
was green and scaly with red eyes, was impressed, said,

"There's not a destroyer of worlds can argue with Manilow."

The phone went. I answered, heard,

"Mr Taylor?"

"Yeah?"

"This is Terry Boyle."

"Like that's supposed to mean something?"

"I spoke to your friend Jeff in Nestor's, about a job."

"Oh yeah, the guy with the suit."

"I hope I'm not interrupting anything."

"You are . . . an episode of *Angel*."

"Are you serious?"

"You bet. I just watched *Buffy*."

"Oh."

"So, what do you want?"

"I need your help."

"I'm already on something."

"Could I at least make a pitch?"

"Why not?"

"Perhaps I could buy you lunch. Would the Brasserie at one tomorrow be suitable?"

"OK."

"Thank you, Mr Taylor, you won't regret it."

"I doubt that."

Click.

The credits were rolling on *Angel*. I considered watching *Sky News* but felt fatigue come calling. In bed, for the first time in ages, I felt the faint glimmer of hope. If I could just hang on to this fragile feeling, I might struggle through. Not surprisingly, I dreamt of vampires. The thing was, they all wore the face of Bill Cassell. His usual minder was there, of course, the big guy, and a third man whom I couldn't see. When I replayed the dream again, I thought of those lines from "The Waste Land", the ones about "the third who walks always beside you".

When I woke, I thought I smelled something odd, took me a time to identify it.

Juicy Fruit.

———

I wore the Age Concern suit. No doubt, it had been a decent item once. I choose it for two reasons: because it was cheap and dark. Checked myself in the mirror. I looked like a corpse that the undertaker had failed to help. Wore a white shirt and wool tie. Only accentuated the lousy suit. When I entered the Brasserie, a gorgeous girl approached, asked,

"Table for one?"

"I dunno, I'm supposed to meet a Mr Boyle."

Her face lit up and,

"Oh, Terence."

My heart sank and she added,

"He's at his usual table, over here."

Led me to the centre, beamed,

"Voila."

Terry Boyle stood up, smiled.

"Jack Taylor?"

"Yeah."

I hoped my dourness showed. He put out his hand, said,

"Glad you could make it!"

"Yeah."

He was well built, about six two, blond hair and a fresh complexion. Not good looking but what they call presentable. Dark grey suit that shouted money. His age was in the thirty zone. The first Irish generation to grow up without the spectre of unemployment and emigration, this had given them an ease, a self-confidence and natural assurance.

The opposite of everything I grew up with. They faced the world on equal footing. We'd sneaked into life with a trail of fear, inadequacy, resentment and yes . . . begrudgery. My response was booze. His generation toyed with Hooches. He said,

"Take a seat."

I did, resolving to burn my suit at the first chance. He asked,

"A drink?"

"Some water, maybe."

He nodded and I asked,

"What?"

"I heard you had a . . . you know . . . a problem."

Christ, was there anyone who hadn't heard? I asked,

"You heard where?"

"Superintendent Clancy. He was a friend of the family."

The waitress came, breezed,

"Ready to order, guys?"

"Jack, what would you like?"

"You seem to know the place, I'll follow you."

"The spaghetti is dynamite . . . that OK? Need a starter?"

I shook my head. The start I needed was a triple scotch. He poured water into glasses, said,

"The grub's excellent. You'll be pleased."

"I can hardly wait."

He gave me a searching look, checked over his shoulder, then back to me with,

"I'm gay."

I turned, shouted to the waitress,

"Glass of wine."

Terence was shocked, stammered,

"Oh don't, I didn't mean to set you off."

I laughed, repeated,

"Set me off! What a great expression. I know you all of two minutes, and you seriously think you can set me off."

Jesus, I was shouting. The waitress came with the drink. Placed it in the middle of the table, no man's land. White wine in a long-stemmed glass, beads of moisture clinging to the outside, like precarious aspirations. Terence tried again.

"I didn't mean to . . . blurt out my sexual orientation. But I've found it best to get it in the open from the beginning."

I leaned over, close to his face, asked,

"What makes you think your sexual identity is of the slightest interest to anybody?"

He hung his head. At least I'd stopped shouting, for which we were all grateful. I said,

"You have the wine."

He grabbed it, downed half in a second, said,

"Thank you . . . I mean, could we start over? I think we got off on the wrong foot."

"Sure."

The food came. I'm sure it was delicious, but I could only toy with it. Terence didn't fare much better. I asked,

"Tell me what Clancy said about me."

He pushed the food aside, began,

"It was the time of the teenage suicides, remember?"

As if I could ever forget. I nodded and he continued,

"The Superintendent used to golf with my dad. The suicides were the talk of the town. He said you'd solved it, despite being an almost chronic alcoholic. He said you could really have been something if drink hadn't ruined you."

I looked at him, asked,

"And what, you think that was some kind of recommendation?"

"I went to an agency, they wouldn't touch the case."

"What case?"

"My father was murdered."

"Oh."

"I know who did it."

"Who?"

"His wife."

"What?"

"My stepmother."

"Aw, come on."

"I'm serious. Please, will you just check her out, a preliminary investigation? I'll pay well."

I was now sitting on the steps outside the Augustinian church.
A faint hint of sun was in the sky, and I felt I should acknowledge it. A Romanian woman, two kids in tow, asked me,

"Is this church Catholic?"

"It is."

And they walked away, not looking back. On the wall beside
me was a huge glass case. Our Mother of Perpetual Help used
to reside there. Someone stole her.

Terence had given me a fat envelope stashed with cash. His
stepmother's name was Kirsten, and she lived at the family home
in Taylor's Hill. The father had been found dead in bed of a
heart attack. I said,

"Nothing suspicious there."

Terence had sighed, answered,

"Speed, speed would have accelerated it. He had a history of
coronary trouble."

"Speed?"

"Kirsten's drug of choice."

"Wouldn't an autopsy have shown this?"

"There was no autopsy."

"Why didn't you demand one?"

"I was in New York. When I got back, he was already cremated."

I thought about that, admitted,

"That's odd."

"Wait till you meet Kirsten; you don't know what odd means."

"And I'm to see her how? . . . Just call and ask, 'Did you kill your husband?' "

Terence let his irritation show, said,

"You're the private eye. You're supposed to be good at this."

"Jeez, who's that good?"

He indicated the envelope, said,

"It's what you're being paid for."

I didn't answer right off, let his tone hang between us, then,

"Terence, one time I'm going to mention this."

"What?"

Like he was seriously irritated now. I said,

"Lose the attitude. Don't ever talk to me like I'm the fucking hired help. You do and I'll break your front teeth."

Outside the restaurant, he'd given me his card. It had his name and three phone numbers. I asked,

"What do you do?"

"Software."

"That's an answer?"

"To my generation, the only one."

I let him have that, said,

"OK, but I think this is a waste of your time and money."

He gave me a small smile, said,

"See Kirsten, then we'll talk."

"Your money."

"And don't forget it."

He was gone before I could react.

I'd walked towards Shop Street when I felt a tug on my arm.
Turned to face my mother. She is your original martyr and is
blessed to have me as her drunkard son. The farther down the
toilet I go, the better she appears. My father was a good man,
and she treated him like dirt. When he died, she did her griev-
ing on the grand scale.

Leaped into widow's weeds and spent every hour available at
the church or graveyard, publicly displaying her loss. Her type
usually has a tame cleric in tow. Fr Malachy, a prize asshole, was
her escort for the previous years. I wouldn't have liked him under the best of circumstances, but as her hostage, I out and out
despised him. My last encounter, he'd shouted,

"You'll be the death of your mother."

I waited a beat before,

"Can I have that in writing?"

His face went purple and he gasped,

"Yah pup yah. Hell won't be hot enough till you're in it."

Who says the golden age of the clergy has passed?

My mother said,

"I saw you at the Augustinian. Were you at mass?"

"Hardly."

Her eyes had the usual granite hue. Under that scrutiny, you knew mercy was not ever on the agenda. Sometimes, though, she could whine anew. Like now, she said,

"I never see you, son."

"Ever wonder why?"

"I pray daily for you, offer you at mass."

"Don't bother."

She strived to appear hurt, didn't carry it off and snapped,

"You're my flesh and blood."

My turn to sigh; it was definitely infectious.

"Was there anything else, Mother?"

"You have a hard heart, Jack. Couldn't we have a cup of tea, talk like civilised human beings?"

I looked at my watch, said,

"I'm late for an appointment. I better go."

"I haven't been well."

"I believe that."

"Do you, son?"

"Oh, yeah, you never had a well day your whole miserable life."

Then I was walking away. No doubt, Fr Malachy would receive an earful later. My heart was pounding and I could feel a tremor in my hands. Had to stop and take a breath outside the Imperial Hotel.

A fellah I knew was on his way in, stopped, asked,

"Fancy a pint, Jack?"

There was nothing I wanted more, but I said,

"No thanks, some other time."

"You sure?"

"I think so."

———

Next day, I ditched the suit. Went to the St Vincent de Paul shop and got a blazer, grey slacks and white shirts. Back at the hotel, I tried them on. Not bad and definitely a step up. In the lobby, Mrs Bailey said,

"My! You do look smart."

"You think?"

"Definitely. A new woman?"

"In a way."

"Wait a moment."

She disappeared then returned with a dark knitted tie, said,

"It was my husband's."

"I couldn't."

"Course you could, now hold still."

And she tied it for me, said,

"There, you are a handsome man."

"Thank you."

I caught a bus at the Square. It broke down before Dominic Street and I figured the hell with it, the walk will do me good.

At Nile Lodge, I checked the address Terence Boyle had given me and began the trek up Taylor's Hill. No doubt about it, this was where the cash was. Past the Ardilaun Hotel and I came to Irish gates. A brass plate proclaimed, "St Anselm".

Pushed them open and walked up a long, tree-lined drive. I was struck by the quiet. Like being in the country. Then the house, a three-storey mansion, ivy creeping along the windows. I stood at the front door, rang the bell.

A few minutes later, the door opened. A woman asked, "Yes?"

English accent with an underlay of Irish. She was that

indeterminate age between thirty and forty. Dark hair to her shoulders and a face that should have been pretty but didn't quite achieve it. Maybe because of the eyes, brown with an unnerving stare. Button nose and full mouth. She had the appearance of someone who's recently lost a lot of weight. Not gaunt but definitely stretched. I asked,

"Mrs Boyle?"

She gave me a long focused look, said,

"Yes."

"I'm a friend of your husband's."

"Were."

"Excuse me?"

"Wrong tense, he's dead."

"Oh . . . I am sorry."

"Would you like to come in?"

"Yes, thank you."

I followed her, noticing how her arse bounced. I felt a tiny stir of interest. The house was ablaze with paintings. I don't know were they any good, but they had the sheen of wealth. Led me into a sitting room, all dark wood. A bay window opened out to a large garden. She said,

"Have a seat."

I sank into a well-worn chair, tried to get my mind in gear. She asked,

"Like a drink?"

"Some water, perhaps?"

She had moved to a full bar, now cocked a hip, said,

"I would have taken you for a drinking man."

She managed to coat the *taken* with a sexual undertone. I loosened the tie, said,

"Used to be."

She said,

"Ah . . . I'm going to have a screwdriver."

"What?"

"Vodka and OJ. This time of the day, it cuts the glare."

"I believe you."

She rubbed at her arms a few times. I knew the burn from speed could do that. Watched as she fixed the drink. She had the quick movements of the practised drinker. Held up the bottle, said,

"Stoli."

"I'll take your word for that."

"You watch movies?"

"Sure."

"You see the likes of Julia Roberts, she orders a drink, it's going to be Stoli on the rocks."

"I'll bear it in mind."

She gave a vague smile, not related to humour. Chucked some ice in the glass, then poured the vodka freely. One of my favourite sounds has always been the clash of ice in a drink. But to a dry alcoholic, it's akin to the torment of hell, a signal to despair. She asked,

"How did you know Frank?"

So distracted was I, I'd no idea who she meant till she added,

"My husband . . . the *friend* you've called to see."

"Oh, right . . . we, um . . . go way back."

She nodded, let the rim of the glass tap against her teeth, a grating noise. She said,

"Ah, you must have been at Clongowes with him."

I clutched at the lifeline, agreed,

"Yeah, exactly."

She moved over to the sofa, settled herself, let her skirt ride up along her thigh, said,

"Wrong answer, fellah."

"Excuse me?"

"Frank didn't go to Clongowes."

She didn't appear unduly concerned, moved to the bar, added a splash of vodka, I took a deep breath, said,

"You got me."

She gave a tiny smile, asked,

"But who is it I've got?"

"Jack Taylor."

"Like that's supposed to mean something."

"I'm been paid to check you out."

A slight raising of her eyebrows and,

"For what?"

"See if you killed your husband."

"You're fucking kidding!"

The curse rolling off her tongue easily, then it hit and she said,

"Terry, that little faggot."

I nodded and she said,

"Jeez, you're not too big on client confidentiality."

I stood up, said,

"So, did you do it?"

"Gimme a break."

"That's a no."

I moved towards the door, and she said,

"You have some neck, just call and ask me if I killed my husband."

"It's direct."

She laughed, said,

"You have a phone number, if I decide to confess?"

"Bailey's Hotel."

"That's where you live?"

"Yeah."

"Well, Jack Taylor, you might not be very good at your job, but you have a certain style."

I'd reached the front door when she added,

"You decide to go back on the booze, give me a call."

I gave her my best blank look, as if I'd no idea what she meant. She gave a nasty smile, said,

"I know the signs, and believe me, you'll be back sooner than you think. It's not really *if* you'll drink, only when."

"Screw you, lady."

"You wish."

And she banged the door in my face. I hated that she was right on both counts.

"I loved my friends so much I was in love with them, wanted them to be in love with me. But since life isn't like that, this completely shafted any chance of a significant relationship for longer than I care to think about."

John Ramster, *Ladies' Man*

The following Monday, a second year student got a cappuccino from the deli. It was one of those crisp fine days, not a cloud in the sky. You could almost touch hope in the air. People's spirits lightened and you'd get a howyah, a smile from strangers.

That kind of day.

The student sat on a bench at the Square, sipped at the coffee. A stray wino would approach and ask for

"Price of a cup of tea, sur."

But it wasn't a serious beg, more from habit than necessity. No intimidation in it. Two non-Europeans asked for directions to Social Security. At noon, the bells rang for the Angelus. Down near the Great Southern, two workmen stopped their labours and blessed themselves. That is a rare sight. Not that they ceased working but that they observed the Angelus.

Around 12.15 p.m., a man approached, stood for a second behind the student. Then he took out a gun, put it to the base of the student's head and pulled the trigger. He then turned on his heel and walked towards the top of the Square . . . and disappeared.

As he walked away, he threw the wrapper from his Juicy Fruit on the road.

The guards weren't appealing for witnesses. They had far too many.

All contradictory.

Descriptions ranged from, tall, short, fat, thin.

He had, variously, long hair, black hair, no hair.

Was wearing, a suit, leather jacket, wax jacket, raincoat.

But definitely, old, young, middle-aged.

A photofit issued fit half the male population and wasn't dissimilar to a few women.

Superintendent Clancy intoned,

"This is a horrendous, heinous crime. The gardaí will not cease until the perpetrator is apprehended."

He rambled on about lawlessness, a crisis in society, drugs and a range of vaguely related topics.

Concluded with,

"The gardaí are pursuing a definite line of inquiry."

In other words, they had zilch.

I had gone to ground with a book.

Here's the lengthy title:

Movie Wars: How Hollywood and the media conspire to limit what films we can see.

By Jonathan Rosenbaum.

I was well into it, had almost forgotten how badly I wanted a drink. The phone went. I picked up, said,

"Yeah."

"Jack, it's Bill."

"Hi, Bill."

"I'm calling for a progress report."

"Oh."

"So, what progress?"

"Inquiries are in hand."

Bitter laugh, then,

"You sound like a guard."

"Old habits, eh?"

"Except I don't want to hear that shite."

"It takes time, Bill."

"And who told you to involve that religious fuck, Flood?"

"Nobody told me. You want to find someone, he's the best."

"I'm telling you, keep him the fuck outa my affairs."

I was getting tired of this, said,

"What are you going to do, fire me?"

I could hear his intake of breath, then,

"Don't get fucking smart with me, Jack. You definitely don't want to do that."

"I don't take threats well, Bill."

"Time you learned."

Click.

I tried to go back to the book, but the spell was gone. What I most wanted to do was to go down to Sweeney's and kick the bejaysus out of Bill. I grabbed my jacket and took the hinges off the door. Childish but satisfying.

In St Anthony's Lane, there is a coffee shop. Invisible to most pedestrians, it's run by a Basque. I'd intended asking how he washed up in Galway but had never found the energy. Plus, caution said that Basques don't do probing good. As usual, it was doing a brisk trade. Law clerks from the Courthouse, teachers from the Mercy school, a random student and two Spanish fishermen. The owner said,

"Jacques!"

I don't have the witty reply to this, nor could I remember his
name, so went with,

"How're you doing?"

Lame, right?

Didn't faze him. He said,

"Café con leche, grande."

"Grand."

He lingered, then said,

"I miss *Glenroe*."

A Basque who longed for Wesley Burrows; the world was
indeed on its axis. I'd been in a few weeks back and a group of
students were turning CDs into ashtrays. One of them said,

"Don't worry, it's Garth Brooks."

He had a faded Marilyn Manson badge on his notebook. I
knew the two events were connected, but I couldn't work up the
energy to work it out. The coffee came, and the owner asked,

"Food?"

"No, I'm good."

I stirred the liquid, anticipated the bitter kick. Such times,
I'd have killed for a cigarette, then a scotch.

Then a line.

Then oblivion.

Physically, I shook myself, in an effort to dispel the harpies.
Loreena McKennitt was playing and I let myself bend to the
music. Glanced up to see my mother pass. Old Galwegians always used the lane to reach the abbey.

She was linking Fr Malachy. He, of course, was enveloped in
cigarette smoke. Once in Carol O'Connell's *The Judas Child* I'd
come across

*Her child needed a covert source of facts, the help of a dirty,
backdoor invader, a professional destroyer of private lives, who*

well understood the loathsome workings of the world's worst scum.

So this is motherhood.

I mouthed,
"Amen."

*"Life taught me a long time ago to leave be anything
that's got more teeth than me."*

Daniel Buckman, *The Names of Rivers*

I was in Nestor's, on my second glass of sparkling Galway wa-
ter. That the day would come when an Irish person paid for
water and paid dear is astonishing. Jeff said,

"You're doing well."

"At what?"

"You know, the drinking . . . the cigs . . . the other stuff."

I shook my head, said,

"I'm flapping against the wind."

He stopped polishing a glass, looked up, asked,

"What does that mean?"

"I'm biting a bullet, and I'm sick of the taste of metal in my
mouth."

He put down the glass, leaned on the counter, said,

"Very poetic if a little ominous."

"Whoever said the clean life would help you live longer was
right. They neglected to add you'd feel every boring minute."

"It'll get easier, Jack."

"I wish I could believe that."

Jeff had been sober for twenty years. Then, riding on a low
after the baby's birth, he'd gone on the batter. A one-night

rampage. I'd been the one to rein him in. A drunk for the de-
fence, he'd been back on track since. I asked,

"Ever feel the need to blow again?"

"Sure."

"That's it . . . sure?"

"No point in dwelling on it, Jack. I can't drink, end of story."

I sort of hated him then. Not in a ferocious fashion but the
dull ache that sickness feels for recovery. I pushed the water away
and got up to leave. Jeff said,

"Cathy's been surfing the net, trying to track down that information you wanted. She hasn't had any luck yet."

"OK, take it easy." I was leaving when the sentry spoke to
me; I nearly dropped from surprise, as he almost never did. He
said,

"You're investigating the Magdalen? Well, I remember it well.
When we were kids, we'd pass by there and see them working in
the gardens. God forgive me, but we called them names and
jeered them. The nuns were standing over the poor bitches like
wardens. I remember they had leather straps, and we got our
kicks thinking about them walloping the girls. Did you know
that when the public finally knew what was going on, the outcry
was so great that in the middle of the night, the bodies of dead
Maggies were exhumed and whisked off to the cemetery to be
buried? There's a mass grave there with all the nameless girls
below."

He took a deep breath, and I offered to buy him a pint. He
said yes but not to expect any more talk; that was his week's ration. I left, visualising the dead girls that were never claimed.

I was heading towards the hotel when a BMW pulled up.
A man got out, said,

"Jack Taylor?"

He was definitely the largest man I'd ever seen. At garda

training at Templemore, I'd seen some of the biggest the country can produce. The midlands in particular yielded men who'd
give new meaning to the term massive. Oddly enough, they
made lousy cops. This guy towered above me. His head was
bald, adding to his menace. Dressed in a white tracksuit, he eyed
me with derision. What else could I reply but,

"Who's asking?"

He stretched out his hand and literally flung me into the car,
then crowded in beside me. Said,

"Bill would like a word."

With his bulk, there wasn't a whole lot of room. I was jammed
up against him, said,

"I hope you showered."

"Shut your mouth."

I did.

They took me to Sweeney's. Ominously, not a customer in
the pub. The giant pushed me ahead, said,

"Bill's in the cellar."

Bill was wearing a boiler suit, said,

"Don't want to get my clothes dirty."

A single hard chair in the middle, surrounded by barrels; the
smell of yeast was overpowering. I must have made a face, as
Bill said,

"I'd have thought it was mother's milk to you."

"You'd have thought wrong."

He gave a tight smile, said,

"Always the mouth, Jack; maybe we can do something about
that. Sit down."

"No, thanks."

The giant grabbed my shoulders, shoved me down, tied my
hands and put a blindfold on me. Bill said,

"Casey doesn't like you, Jack."

"Gee . . . that's worrying."

I got a wallop to my left ear. It hurt like a bastard. Bill said,

"Excuse the dramatics, but you don't want to actually see Nev. He's kind of shy. He's a huge fan of *The Deer Hunter* and he likes to play, so I'll talk you through this."

I could smell Juicy Fruit, and the strength of the scent made me want to gag. I heard a gun being cocked, and Bill said,

"You owe me twice, Jack."

"I thought we were working on that."

"But you need to focus, Jack. You're not paying attention. Nev is holding an old revolver 'cause he's an old fashioned guy, and he's put two bullets in there and yes, that sound you hear is him spinning the barrel. OK, folks, here we go; let's play."

The sound of the hammer hitting an empty chamber put the fear of God into me, and I thought I'd pass out. Bill said,

"Gee, lucky."

Sweat rolled into my eyes. I realised I'd bitten my tongue, could taste blood in my mouth. The gun was withdrawn, and Bill said,

"Halfway there, but to hell or salvation? How you doing, Jack?"

I wasn't doing too good.

I said,

"Fuck you, Bill."

"You want me to spin or just go for it?"

The muzzle against my head again, the giant sniggering. I swear he was grinning. Nev thumbed the hammer, fired.

Click on empty.

A tremor shook my whole body. I hadn't vented my bowels but it was close. My teeth were chattering. Bill said,

"Jeez, talk about luck."

I couldn't find my voice and he added,

"I think we've got you focused. Get results real soon, Jack."

And I heard him walk away, Nev talking quietly with him as they went. The giant tilted my chair, and I went face down on the stone floor. Water, beer and God knows what else had pooled together. He untied my hands, pulled the blindfold roughly and spat; then he, too, walked to the stairs.

I pushed myself up and another spasm hit. I leaned against a keg, trying to still my hammering heart. Finally, I moved and I slowly climbed up the stairs. The bar was hopping, almost all the space occupied. No sign of Bill, Nev or the giant. Black dots danced before my eyes and I pushed forward, shouted,

"Large Jameson."

No response. I edged in past a docker who gave me the look. Whatever he saw in my face, he decided to give me room. The barman continued to ignore me. I shouted,

"Gimme a bloody Jameson."

He stopped, grinned, said,

"You had your shots; now you're barred."

Guffaws from the crowd. I slunk out of there with my soul in ribbons. Wouldn't you know, the weather had picked up, an almost bright sun, high in the sky. A man passing, said,

"Isn't it great to be alive?"

I had no answer. Least none that didn't require fisticuffs.

Pure rage can operate on either of two levels. There's the hot, smouldering, all-encompassing kind that instantly lashes out. Seeking immediate annihilation. There's the second that comes from a colder place. Fermented in ice, it withdraws upon itself, feeding on quiet ferocity for a suitable occasion. This is the deadliest.

Most of my battered life, I'd been afflicted with the second, and with dire consequences. As I watched the sun bounce off the water, I submerged in this. The claws of patience sucking deep into my psyche felt as dangerous as I'd ever felt.

Such times, to stir the cauldron, my mind seizes on a mantra to keep the madness corralled. A mental front to help me function as the fires are built within. There is never rhyme or reason to the chant. My subconscious throws up some non-related barrier to maintain my mobility. When I'd been discharged from the guards, I'd had one session with a psychiatrist and outlined the above.

He said,

"You're bordering on pathological psychosis."

I'd stared at him for full five minutes, then answered,

"That's what I was hoping for."

He'd offered a course of tranquillizers, and to that I'd given him my police smile. The one that says,

"Watch your back."

As I turned from the docks and walked towards Merchant's Road, the mantra began.

Hannibal Lector's words to Clarice Starling in the dungeon for the criminally insane:

You are an ambitious, hustling little rube. Your eyes shine like cheap shoes but you have some taste, a little taste.

Over and over, those words played, and I was back at the hotel before I realised. A homeless person approached, and I mechanically handed over some money. He wasn't pleased, asked,

"That's all you got?"

I turned to him, touched his shoulder, said,

"I've some taste, a little taste."

He took off like that bat out of Meatloaf's hell.

———

In my room, I'd lain on the bed, fully clothed, and shut my eyes. Not sleep or even a close approximation but a trancelike state that pulled me down to an area of nonconsciousness. Teetering on catatonia, I remained thus till darkness fell.

When I came to, the fear had fallen away. I acknowledged a hard granite-like lump lodged beside my heart and said,

"The show must go on."

I was sitting on the bed, trying to read, couldn't concentrate, so put it aside.

I headed for Nestor's. The sentry was in position, gave me a look and said,

"Watch out."

He did an unheard of thing. He actually moved stools, away from me. I could only guess at how hostile was the vibe I was transmitting. Jeff said,

"How's it going, Jack?"

His expression said,

"I'm not sure I want the answer."

I gave a slow smile, said,

"Couldn't be better. Can I get something?"

"Sure . . . coffee OK?"

"No . . . it's not, . . . I'd like a large Jameson."

He looked round as if help was available. It wasn't. He asked,

"You sure that's a good idea?"

"Did I miss something, Jeff? I could have sworn I asked for a drink, not your opinion."

He wiped at his mouth, then,

"Jack, I can't."

I stared into his eyes, took my time, said,

"You're refusing to serve me?"

"C'mon, Jack, I'm your friend. You don't want to do this."

"How on earth would you know what I want to do? If I re-call, when you went on the piss, I didn't get righteous on you."

I turned to leave, and he called,

"Jack, wait up, Cathy has some news for you."

I shouted over my shoulder.

"I have news for Cathy: I don't give a fuck."

Outside, I gulped air, trying to calm my adrenaline, muttered,

"Great, you've just hurt your best friends. How smart was that?"

The off-licence was jammed with under-age drinkers. Cider, vodka and Red Bull were definitely the drug of choice. The guy behind the counter was in his bad thirties. Whatever bitter pill he'd had to swallow, it was still choking him. With-out looking at me, he grunted,

"What?"

"A bit of civility for openers."

His head came up, and he asked,

"What?"

"Bottle of Jameson."

I was going to add,

"Quickly."

But let it slide.

As he wrapped, he said,

"You think I should ask for ID?"

I knew he meant the line of teenagers, but before I could re-ply, he said,

"If I refuse, I get my windows smashed."

I gave him the money and said,

"The guards can shut you down."

"Like they give a toss."

I was walking along the bottom of Eyre Square. Under a street lamp, a woman in a shawl asked,

"Some change, mister?"

She was one of those Mediterranean gypsies who stalked the fast food joints. Her mouth was a riot of gold teeth. The light threw a malevolent shape to her silhouette. I thought,

"What the hell?"

And reached in my pocket. Didn't have a single coin. Had left my change on the counter. I said,

"Sorry, I'm out."

"Give me something."

"I told you, I'm tapped."

She eyed the brown bag, pointed, and I said,

"Dream on."

I moved past her and she hissed. I turned back. She was literally standing on my shadow. Throwing her head back, she drew saliva from the core of her being, spat on that dark shape, said,

"You will always break bread alone."

I wanted to break her neck, but she moved fast away. I am no more superstitious than your average Irish guilt-ridden citizen. Using my shoe, I tried to erase the stain her spittle had left on the pavement. Nearly dropped the bottle, muttered,

"Now that would be cursed."

———

Luc Sante in *Low Life* wrote:

The night is the corridor of history, not the history of famous people or great events, but that of the marginal, the ignored, the suppressed, the unacknowledged; the history of vice, of fear, of confusion, of error, of want, the history of intoxication, of vainglory, of delusion, of dissipation, of delirium. It strips off the city's veneer of progress and modernity and civilization and reveals the wilderness.

I said "Amen" to that.

Outside the hotel, I noticed a very impressive car. An elderly man was staring at it. He said,

"That's an S–type Jaguar."

"Is it yours?"

"No such luck."

His eyes were shining as they took in the sleek black body. He said,

"The thing is, with all the power and luxury of a 3–litre V65–type at your disposal, even your business miles are positively a pleasure."

He sounded like a commercial. I said,

"You sound like a commercial."

He gave a shy smile, said,

"That baby doesn't need a commercial."

I made to move by and he said,

"Do you know how much that costs?"

"A lot, I should imagine."

I could almost see the cash register in his eyes. He said,

"You'd need half a decent Lotto."

I let out a low whistle, said,

"That's got to be a lot."

He gave me a look of bordering contempt, said,

"No, that is a lot of car!"

I went into the hotel, moving quickly to avoid reception. Not quite fast enough, as Mrs Bailey called,

"Mr Taylor."

"Yeah."

"You have a visitor."

"Oh."

I went into the lobby. Kirsten was sitting in a chair by the open fire. Dressed in black jeans, black sweater and long dark coat, she looked like trouble. Seeing me, she said,

"Surprise."

The heat reflected on her cheeks gave her a high colour, as if she was excited. Maybe she was. She saw the bottle in my hand, said,

"Party for one?"

"Yeah."

She stood up, and I hadn't realised how tall she was. A smile as she said,

"Not a good idea to drink alone."

"How would you know?"

"Oh, I know."

The smart thing would have been to say,

"Hop it."

When did I ever get to do the smart thing? I said,

"My room's not much."

Again the smile with,

"What makes you think I was expecting much?"

The elevators at Bailey's have a life of their own. The only thing reliable about them is their unreliability. I pushed the button, said,

"This could take a while."

"Stop bragging."

Mrs Bailey smiled at us from the desk. I nodded and Kirsten said,

"She likes me."

I turned to look at her, said,

"Don't be so sure."

"Oh, I am sure. I worked at it."

"Is that what you do, you get people to like you?"

"Only some people."

I couldn't resist, asked,

"What about me?"

"That doesn't need any work. You like me already."

"Don't count on it."

"I have."

The elevator arrived with a grinding of metal. I pulled the door open, asked,

"Want to risk it?"

"I insist on it."

Naturally the space was cramped, and we were jammed together. I could smell her perfume, asked,

"Is that patchouli?"

"Yes."

"Old hippies never die."

She looked into my eyes, said,

"I guess that's the bottle against me or else you're happier to see me than you're saying."

There's probably a reply to this. I didn't have it.

"It is not an arbitrary decree of God but in the nature of man, that a veil shuts down on the facts of tomorrow; for the soul will not have us read any other cipher but that of cause and effect."

Ralph Waldo Emerson, *Essays,* "Heroism"

I flicked on the television, one of those moments, if not God- given, at least God-inspired. Henry, in the eighty-second minute, scored a magnificent header against Spartak. Almost simultaneously with me switching on, he walloped it home. I said, awestruck,

"Fuck."

She sat on the bed, said,

"Which means you're pleased?"

"Oh yeah."

She took a moment, looked at the screen, said,

"Too bad about Leeds."

"They lost?"

"Yes."

"You follow football?"

"I follow men."

Gave me a smile that was unreadable. She looked round the room, said,

"Somewhat sparse."

"I'm a simple guy."

"No, Jack, whatever else, you're not simple. Drunks never are."

I still had the bottle in my hand. Her remark stung, all the more for its bitter truth. She caught on, asked,

"Ah, did I hit a nerve?"

I got two glasses from the bathroom, rinsed them, handed one over, asked,

"What do you want?"

"Pour."

I did.

She patted the bed, said,

"Don't be shy."

I took a chair on the opposite side of the room, raised my glass, said,

"*Sláinte.*"

"Whatever."

No doubt she was one attractive woman.

I took a sip of the whiskey. Ah, it was if I'd never been away. Kirsten asked,

"Been a while, has it?"

"Yeah."

I knocked back the rest, wanting that warmth to hit my stomach. She reached in her bag, produced a small clear cellophane bag, said,

"I brought you a present, in case you weren't drinking or even if you were."

Tossed the cocaine to me. I didn't make any attempt to catch, let it fall short and to the floor. She didn't seem, to care, said,

"Tell me about coke."

I could do that, said,

"Charlie and the Music Factory, except it finally takes away the music. I think I like George Clooney's remark best. 'It would dress you up for a party and never take you there.' "

She digested this, then,

"You must know about punding."

I wasn't sure I'd heard her correctly. After a spell on the wagon, the first one drives hard.

"Punding . . . no, I don't know."

"You start something then keep returning to the start, over and over again. It's what cocaine causes."

I let out a breath, said,

"There you have it, the story of my life. Would I be called a pundit?"

She laughed out loud. A wonderful sound. When a woman does that, without inhibition, without caring how it appears, she is truly lovable. She said,

"Tell me more."

"In the beginning, coke makes you love yourself. For me, that was a whole other mind fuck. Plus, it gives you a rush of such power. It shrinks the supply of blood to the eyes and makes you bright-eyed. I once saw Mick Houghton interviewed."

I stood up, could already feel the booze in my legs, got the bottle, poured another, offered it to Kirsten. She said,

"No, I'm good. Who's Mick Houghton?"

"He was PR to Echo and the Bunnymen, Julian Cope, Elastica."

She gave me a look of profound disbelief, went,

"How do you know this stuff?"

"Yeah, scares me, too."

"It should."

"Anyway, he said, 'Coke's worse than heroin. Heroin kills you whereas coke destroys you. People can kick smack before it kills them so that their careers might at least remain intact. You can't say that about coke.' "

She rose from the bed, moved to pick up the cellophane, said,

"You won't be needing this then?"

"No."

The phone rang. I picked up, said,

"Yeah?"

"Jack, it's Cathy."

Instantly, guilt consumed me, for my behaviour towards Jeff. I hoped the whiskey didn't sound in my voice. I said,

"Cathy."

"I got the information you wanted."

"That's great . . . I'll pay you, of course."

"I don't think so."

The tone of her voice was flat, cold. I said,

"I was a little out of line earlier."

"So what else is new, Jack?"

"I'll come by tomorrow."

"Don't bother. I left the envelope with Mrs Bailey."

Click.

Kirsten said,

"Romantic spat?"

"Not exactly."

She moved to the door, said,

"I hate to drink and run but . . ."

"You're going?"

"What were you expecting? Drinks and a fast fuck."

The word echoed harsh in the room. I tried to get a grip, asked,

"What did you come for?"

She feigned huge surprise, said,

"To touch base, see how your investigation was going."

I searched for a sarcastic rejoinder, something to lash her with. Nothing came, and she said,

"Why don't you just ask me?"

"Ask you what?"

"If I killed my husband."

I finished my drink. Could feel it move behind my eyes, asked,

"Did you kill your husband?"

She gave a laugh of pure delight, said,

"Ah . . . that would be telling. Keep it in your pants, Jack."

And she was gone.

I stood in the middle of the room, shouted,

"What was that about?"

The bottle, three quarters full, stood on the dresser. What sanity I had said,

"So, OK . . . you've had two drinks, no real damage done. We're not talking major damage. Go to bed. In the morning, start over."

I seriously considered all of that for a full minute, then I said, "Fuck it."

What I thought about was Raymond Chandler and what he once said:

How do you tell a man to go away in hard language? Scram, beat it, take off, take the air, hit the road, and so forth. All good enough. But give me the classic expression actually used by Spike O'Donnell (of the O'Donnell brothers of Chicago, the only small outfit to tell the Capone mob to go to hell and live). What he said was, Be Missing.

All I need to say about the rest of the night is . . . I wrote a poem.

God forgive me.

Drinking whiskey has led me down so many dark streets,

exposed me to situations that were horrific and produced medieval hangovers. But in our long chequered relationship. I'd never descended to the level of poetry.

Could I remember penning it?

Course not.

The writing was all over sheets of blotched paper. Thankfully, a part of it was unreadable, simply an illegible scrawl. But the bones were there. I could recall sitting on the bed, remembering my London wedding. We'd got hitched in a registry office at Waterloo. How fitting that was.

Our nuptial night had ended in a blazing row. I'd surfaced the next morning, blitzed and alone in a cheap hotel near the Arches.

Here is the poem.

In all its feckless glory.

Wasted in Waterloo

And smooth as silk
The cheapest type, all flash
If little content
I'd sipped on early drinks
Till later then
Crawling on my bed
I slow chugged
Flatter cans of lager
And under scattered socks
The crumpled suit, had
Chased an aspirin
Amid
The debris, found
Your confusing words, cast-off
I fell off

The bed
To evening
This . . . this heavy Waterloo
After opening time perhaps
Behind a gin or four
I'll dare again
Bit-o-breeze
Dance through your wedding vows.

Asked myself,

"What the hell is this?"

But I didn't bin it. Folded it with care and put it in the introduction to Francis Thompson's *The Hound of Heaven*.

Where else did it belong?

Only then did I notice my knuckles. Torn and bleeding. I hadn't left the room. Christ, I prayed I hadn't. My stomach was churning, as if I'd drunk battery acid. A mother of a headache, sweat leaking into my eyes, plus the almighty thirst. Went to the bathroom for water and solved one mystery. The mirror was cracked, and obviously with some force.

Heard intermittent groans and realised I was making them. Course, I'd passed out in my clothes. Boy, did they stink. Tore them off and stepped gingerly into the shower. Got it to scalding and roared like a penitent. Endured it as long as I could. My mind wasn't thinking,

"No more drinking."

It was already visualising a cold pint of lager, beads of moisture on the glass. Heard my door open and someone enter. My pounding heart went into overdrive. Wrapped a towel round me, looked out. Janet, the chambermaid, was looking older than Mrs Bailey but refused to retire. Now, she was standing amid the debris, shaking her head.

I said,

"Janet, it's OK . . . I'll tidy up."

"But, Mr Taylor, what happened? You're usually so tidy."

I wanted to shout,

"Leave the fucking room, all right. You're waiting for an explanation; Christ . . . you're the chambermaid . . . Gimme a break."

Could I afford to trample on yet another person's feelings, especially as she was a gentle soul? Had once given me a rosary beads. Now I wanted to strangle her with them. What I said was,

"Bit of a celebration, Arsenal beat Spartak."

She looked right at me, said,

"Ah, Mr Taylor, you're back on the beer."

Serious rage boiled in me but I tried,

"Just a few friends in, nothing too boisterous."

"Says you! Look at this place."

This was so unlike her. Normally, she wouldn't comment on an earthquake. When you're dying with a hangover, the whole world gets a hard on. I said,

"JANET . . . LEAVE IT."

"No need to raise your voice, Mr Taylor, I'm not deaf."

And she began to back out, paused to add,

"I'm going to pray to Matt Talbot for you."

I managed to drink half a cup of coffee and only throw up once. Put on clean jeans and fresh white shirt. What that did was make me appear hungover in new gear. At reception, Mrs Bailey said,

"A letter for you, Mr Taylor."

I put out my left hand so she wouldn't see my torn knuckles. I said,

"It's from Cathy."

"Now there's a lovely girl."

"She is."

Mrs Bailey paused, obviously comparing her to Kirsten of the night before, then,

"I get the impression, Mr Taylor, that Cathy is a little cross with you."

What could I say . . . join the queue?

I nodded, attempting to appear contrite. Not difficult when you're dying anyway. Outside, I stuffed the letter in my pocket as my system threatened to upchuck anew.

The Magdalen

The girls were huddled under the bedclothes, trying to keep warm and to give each other some meagre comfort. They heard the sound of heels and then the bedclothes were whipped away. The woman they called Lucifer screamed, "What unnatural act are you whores performing?"

She grabbed the first girl by the hair and punched her in the mouth. Then reaching for the second, she pulled her down to the toilets, forced a bar of soap into her mouth and said,

"Chew, chew if you don't want to get the hiding of your life."

The girl, blinded by tears and terror, began to chew.

I began to walk towards the Great Southern. I knew the porter there. As I came through the revolving doors, he said,

"Rough night, Jack?"

"Yeah."

"None of us getting any younger."

I palmed him a few notes, said,

"Get us a pint and a half one."

The Southern, of course, is not an early house. Good Lord, God forbid. It does have a huge lobby with secluded corners. If you need a cure in tranquil seclusion, you won't do better.

Had just slunk down in a vast armchair when a man appeared. I thought it was my drinks. No . . . Brendan Flood. He said,

"I saw you come in."

"Not now . . . OK?"

"I have the information you require."

I was about to tap the envelope and say,

"Me, too."

But he sat down.

What I most didn't want was him seeing me on the booze and first thing of a morning. Everything was down the toilet.

The porter came and seemed surprised I'd company. All our eyes locked on the tray of drinks. Before I could launch into some half-assed lame story, Brendan said,

"Same for me."

The porter gave us a look of confusion, asked,

"You guys celebrating something?"

Brendan snapped,

"Get the drinks, all right."

The porter slunk off, and I asked Brendan,

"You're serious?"

He nodded and I probed,

"You're drinking?"

He stared at me, said,

"I don't think you're the one to recriminate."

"I'm not . . . I'm . . . surprised."

The porter returned, and Brendan put a mess of notes on the tray and said,

"Keep the change."

If he was grateful, he hid it well. Brendan grabbed the shot, drained it, then followed with most of the pint. He sat back, closed his eyes, said,

"This is the best bit."

Who was I to argue? Did the same with my drinks but stopped short of the eye closing. I like to see it coming. An overwhelming compulsion for nicotine landed. You open the door of one addiction and all the outriders gallop behind. Brendan reached in his jacket, took out a packet of Major. Yer legitimate coffin nails. Popularised by Robbie Coltrane in *Cracker*.

He shook one loose, produced a kitchen box of matches and fired up. I asked,

"Can I?"

Enveloped in smoke, he waved a hand, yes. The cigarette felt odd in my mouth, and the first few pulls were godawful. I stubbed it out. He gave a malevolent grin, said,

"Par for the course. The first is shite, but you'll be puffing good-oh in jig time."

I didn't argue. My own sorry existence was proof of his theory. I waited a beat, said,

"What happened, Brendan?"

He took a deep breath, said,

"The Magdalen is what happened."

I let him take his time, didn't push, and finally he ran his fingers through his hair and began,

"I found a woman in the Claddagh, in her seventies, who was one of the inmates. At first she wouldn't talk about it, but then she heard I go to prayer meetings and she agreed to tell. The first thing you ought to know is this woman was absolutely terrified. The laundry has been closed for years, but it still reaches out to her. There was a woman there the girls called Lucifer, a lay person the nuns employed to help out. She was the devil incarnate, beating the girls, shaving their heads, scouring them for lice."

He paused, lit a cig, and I saw the tremor in his hand. He asked,

"Any idea of how to clean lice from the body?"

"No, no I don't."

"Me neither, but I'll never forget now. You immerse the person in scalding water and then pour carbolic acid in; you have to be real careful lest you flay the creature alive. I believe it stings like a bastard. Lucifer was an expert at the dosage and delighted in the process. She'd let the girls know days before so they'd be good and frightened. Not all of the girls were unmarried mothers; some were put there for disobedience to their parents. In an era of dire poverty, it was one less mouth to feed.

"My witness remembers two girls who were friends. One

was there for unwanted pregnancy, but the other had simply been accused of stealing. Lucifer took particular delight in tormenting those two, would tell them that God had forsaken them, and the only thing those girls had was a simple faith. The she-devil systematically eroded that. She used a blunt scissors to hack off the tresses of one and refused to allow the other to wash so she stank to high heaven, if you'll excuse the pun. All those girls had was each other, no hope of any life after, with just misery every single day, and if you separated them, then they were doomed. Lucifer went a step further and persuaded one that the other had betrayed her. The girl hanged herself a few days later. With constant taunting from the woman, the second drank bleach they used in the laundry. Now if you have ever seen someone who has drunk bleach, maybe in your days on the force, you'll know it takes days of utter agony to die. Five days to die in the most appalling conditions, with Lucifer telling her the fires of hell, which already had her friend, were being stoked up for her arrival."

The sweat was pouring down his forehead, and he turned, stared at me, asked,

"Do you know what those two innocents were?"

"No."

"Martyrs, the real thing, dying in agony for love. Magdalen Martyrs. And if I fucking believed in anything any more, I'd pray for the poor souls. I swear I dream about them every night. Them nuns in that place, you know why they hated the girls so much. This is only my own theory but it works: it's because those girls had experienced the one thing they'd never know, sex . . . or if you wanted to push, love."

Brendan said,

"I need more drink, but I don't think I could stomach that porter again."

Then he was up and gone. I didn't know if he'd return.

He did, bearing a tray ablaze with drink. Enough to get a small rugby team blitzed. I said,

"That cost a bit."

He sat down heavily, said,

"It's only money, who gives a fuck?"

I'd never heard him swear. This was the man who attended prayer meetings where they spoke in tongues. A man who chastised me if I as much as muttered "damn". He lashed in more booze, belched, said,

"I'm fucked."

I waited. He lit another Major, said,

"My wife left me."

"Oh."

I was going to say, "Hey, mine left me, too," but felt he wasn't looking for identification, so I waited. He said,

"She went to England and then came back. She's in the house but doesn't talk one word to me."

I tried to find some platitude, found none. He continued,

"After I left the guards, I was lost. You know that deal, Jack . . . yeah."

I nodded.

"Like you, Jack, I could have become a drunk, but I was saved. God spoke to me. The void within was filled."

Then he stopped, drank some more. So I asked,

"You were happy?"

"Happy! I was bloody ecstatic. Like being high all the time."

More drink, then,

"But lately, all the things I see, the awfulness of life, the lousy, sordid daily grind of most people's lives, my belief began to ebb. I was found and now I'm lost. How can you believe in a God who lets those girls die?"

I took a cig and, yeah, the second one wasn't half bad. I said,

"Maybe it's just a phase . . . you know, your faith will return."

He shook his head violently, near spat,

"Naw, I'm done with all that. The prayer group I attended, bunch of hypocrites."

Anger rolled off him in waves. He said,

"Then the Magdalen, I began to investigate for you. What was done to those poor women, treated like slaves and in the name of religion. My advice to you is, let it go. It will taint you, too."

I took out Cathy's envelope, opened it and written there was,

Rita Monroe

17 Newcastle Road.

No phone number, no relatives traced.

Before I could share this, a man in a morning suit appeared, said,

"Gentlemen, I'm afraid I'll have to ask you to take your custom elsewhere."

Brendan looked up. Drunk and belligerent, he asked,

"Who the fuck are you? And where did you get the bloody suit?"

"Please, I must ask you to lower your voice. Guests are not accustomed to such early morning . . . boisterousness."

Brendan stood up, shouted,

"Once were . . . guards."

I grabbed his arm, said,

"Come on, I know a place."

He took a swing at the manager, who ducked, and I managed to drag Brendan out to the street. The fresh air hit him like revelations and he staggered, said,

"Maybe some coffee."

"Good idea."

I took him back to Bailey's. Got him into an armchair. Mrs Bailey came over, asked,

"What happened to him?"

"Bad news."

"I see."

But she didn't. What she saw was a ravaged drunk. I said,

"If I could get some coffee . . . Then probably a cab."

She gave us another look, then turned away. Brendan asked,

"Are we in Dublin?"

"What?"

"I'm kidding. I'm not that far gone."

"You tried to deck the manager at the Southern."

"That wasn't drink; that was necessity."

He did seem improved. There was no sign of the coffee. I asked,

"Are you going to be OK?"

"What do you think, Jack?"

A horrible thought occurred to me and I asked,

"Brendan, you wouldn't, you know . . . do something stupid?"

He turned to stare at me, said,

"You mean, top myself?"

I nodded and he said,

"Dante's second level of hell is reserved for suicides."

"Is that an answer?"

He touched my shoulder, said,

"Jack."

"I might need your word on this."

He didn't answer, and Mrs Bailey came, said,

"I called a taxi."

Brendan stood, said,

"I suppose that means our session is over."

"I'll come with you if you want, keep you company."

"No, I'll be fine."

And he was gone.

Mrs Bailey, standing behind me, said,

"I didn't forget the coffee, but all it gives you is a wide-awake drunk."

I had no answer for her. No civil one anyway. Went up to my room and collapsed on the bed, was out in seconds.

I had a dream where I went to Zhivago Records. Declan, of course, was in attendance and sold me the complete back catalogue of REM. Nightmare indeed. Behind the counter was a girl whose hair had been shorn, and she asked me where could she buy some bleach. As the dream wavered, I swear I could hear, clear as day, Stipe singing "Losing My Religion".

"The difference between an alcoholic and a heavy drinker is an alcoholic believes his flaws are sincere but his virtues are fake. A heavy drinker keeps his virtues for himself and cripples others with his flaws."

Phyl Kennedy, *Where Am I Now When I Need Me?*

The next few days were hell personified. Hangover supreme.
Spent them mostly on, under, across the bed. All the while, the booze calling,

"Come, let us fix you."

Yeah.

At one stage, I came to with the sheets in a noose round my neck. Did not want to ever analyse that. On the bureau was a small photo. Was I hallucinating? Blinked twice but it remained. Approached slowly. It was of a man in a cheap tweed suit, suffering writ large on his face. At the bottom, I read,

"Matt Talbot."

Crept back to bed after turning the photo face down. Next time I surfaced, it was gone. I would never ask Janet about it. Could only hope she was the culprit . . . *ELSE?*

Third, fourth day, weak as a kitten, I showered, put on fresh clothes. I felt more fragile than a whisper. My mind locked on whiskey, I headed for a café on Prospect Hill. Ordered scrambled eggs, toast and tea. The table swam before my eyes and sweat cruised my body. If I could get some nourishment . . .

Months before, on my previous case, I'd been deep into

coke. Ran out and panicked. Cathy, in her punk days, knew all the drug players. I'd leaned heavily on our friendship and gotten the name of a dealer. It bruised our relationship, but coke recognises no loyalties.

I'd gone to meet "Stewart" and scored. He was far from the stereotype. Lived in a neat house near the college, and if he resembled anyone, it was a banker. What kept him successful, unnicked and unknown was a low profile.

I pushed the breakfast away, couldn't eat. The waitress asked,

"Was there something wrong?"

Was there ever, but not with the food. I even put the tea aside, said,

"No . . . I'm not feeling well."

She gave me a motherly smile, said,

" 'Twill be that stomach bug, the whole town's got it."

I walked to the canal, alternating hot and cold, praying Stewart was home. Knocked on the door, waited a minute, then he opened, said,

"Yes?"

"Stewart, I dunno if you remember me?"

The sharp eyes opened, then,

"Cathy's friend . . . don't tell me . . . it's John Taylor."

"Jack."

You have to ask, do you want drug dealers to remember your name? He said,

"Come in."

The house was spotless, like a showplace. Stewart was wearing pressed chinos, a white shirt, loosely knotted tie. He offered me a seat, asked,

"Tea, coffee, pharmaceuticals?"

"You wouldn't have a cigarette?"

That old craving suddenly surfaced. He gave a measured laugh, said,

"The corner shop would be the place. I don't allow smoking in the house."

Sure enough, on the wall was a decal with

SMOKE FREE ZONE

I said,

"You're kidding."

"Foul habit."

"Stewart, you're a drug dealer . . . come on."

He raised a finger, said,

"I'm a businessman. I never indulge."

"Pretty flexible set of morals you got there, pal."

He spread his palms, said,

"Works for me. But I don't think you dropped by for a debate on ethics, did you?"

"No, you're right. I need some major tranquillizers. I'm really hurting."

He tilted his head, like a doctor, asked,

"What have you been using . . . or abusing? I'm never quite sure of the terminology."

"I am. Abusing is when you're fucked."

"Aptly put. I shall remember the distinction. Excuse me."

He went upstairs. I looked round. If there'd been a drinks cabinet, I'd have *abused* it. When he returned, he was carrying a briefcase, asked,

"How much are you planning to spend?"

"As much as it takes."

Big smile, everything to do with money and no relation to

humour. He laid a series of small plastic bottles on the table, said,

"You'll notice red, blue, yellow and black caps."

"Accessorised?"

Gave me a vexed look, said,

"You'd do well to pay attention."

"I'll try."

"Red are powerful painkillers, the yellow are mega tranks, blue are Quaaludes and black . . ."

He gave a deep sigh of admiration, continued,

"Are black beauties!"

I asked,

"Could I have some water?"

"Now?"

"No, next Tuesday . . . come on."

When he went to fetch it, I flipped the lid off the red, dry swallowed two. He returned with the water, and I gulped it down, the tremor in my hand like a flag. He said,

"For what it's worth, I advise extreme caution with all of these."

"Like a government health warning."

He took out a tiny calculator, did the sums, presented the screen to me. I said,

"Jesus, I'd need the major tranquillizers."

I laid out a mini-hill of bills and he said,

"For cash customers only, I throw in a little something special."

"I doubt if it's humour."

He produced a small brown bottle, asked,

"What do you know about GHB?"

"Grievous bodily harm?"

"Not in the sense you mean. It's alias 'liquid E' and it is a

painkiller. Within twenty minutes of downing it, your movements, control, vision and brain become impaired. Inhibitions,
clothes, self-control disappear. It doesn't have the rush of E. Do
you want to know how they hit on it, if you'll excuse the pun?"

He had a feverish glint to his eyes. Now I knew where he
lived, . . . pharmacology. I said,

"Hit me."

"It was first manufactured as an experimental anaesthetic
and aid to childbirth. It relaxes the muscles. Alas, it was banned
in America because it caused seizures. Then it became linked
to Rohypnol, the date rape number. Its big plus is the morning
after. It leaves you perky and alert."

"I like this already."

He held the bottle up, said,

"Now for the downer. Mess with the dosage and you can go
into a coma. Taken properly, it gives you euphoria and libido.
Listen carefully . . . are you listening?"

The two reds I'd popped couldn't possibly be kicking in yet,
but I was definitely on the mend, said,

"I'm rapt."

"OK, here are the rules. Never mix with alcohol or any
other chemicals. Always take the right dosage. Wait forty minutes between doses. Let somebody know what you're doing.
On no account drive a car."

"Got it."

"You certain?"

"Yeah."

He added the bottle to the other goodies. He sat back, gave
me a long look, and I went,

"What?"

"You know, Jack . . . you don't mind if I call you Jack, do
you?"

"It's my name, just don't wear it out."

His eyes lit and he said,

"Don't tell me . . . Robert De Niro to Ed Harris in . . . shit, what is the film?"

The pills had hit big time, and I was almost warming to him. As I couldn't recall the movie either, I smiled enigmatically. He said,

"OK, that's cool, it will come to me. Anyway, I was going to say, despite your smart mouth . . . and boy, do you ever have that . . . I have a sneaking regard for you."

I was full tilt boogie now, said,

"Glad to hear it."

He was on his feet, saying,

"Tell you what I'm going to do."

I waited. Shit, I felt so fine, I'd have waited a week. He said,

"I'm going to Vike you."

I didn't know was this some sex thing or had I simply misheard. He went,

"Vicodin is a prescription painkiller. It's Vike that kept Matthew Perry in rehab."

"Who?"

"You don't know *Friends*?"

"I've seen *Buffy*."

He waved that aside, continued,

"It's the drug of choice for rappers, rockers and the A-list. Eminem has a tattoo of the ovoid shape on his arm. He even put a graphic of Vike on 'Slim Shady'."

I was lost, if happily so. On he went.

"An American psychologist characterised the average Vike user as having all the attributes of the economic winner today . . . agility, problem solving, system application. It's a bastard to get supplies of, but I'm expecting a delivery soon, and your name goes on the list."

"Thanks, Stewart."

He stared at me, so I figured it was time to go. I stood up, wanting to glide, said,

"It's been a time."

"Stay in touch, Jack, for the Vike vibe."

"Gotcha."

He put my purchases in a McDonald's bag and let me out. For the sheer novelty of a pain free walk, I headed for the River Inn. There is no sign of a river and the canal is a good two miles away. I'd been in here once before. I took a window seat, and a girl in her twenties approached, said,

"Howyah?"

"Great."

"What can I get you?"

"Coffee."

I didn't need a drink; I didn't even want one, just to bask in the glow of the drugs. A man was sitting near me, engrossed in a book. He looked up and nodded. With my fresh bonhomie, I asked,

"What are you reading?"

"The Assassin's Cloak."

"Crime?"

"Good Lord, no. It's an anthology of diarists. You read one entry per day. Everyone from Pepys to Virginia Wolfe."

"Good?"

"Brilliant. I missed a few days, so I'm treating myself to a week's catching up."

And then I remembered Rita Monroe. Went through my pockets and found her address. I was practically in the neighbourhood. Outside, I could feel a second wave of elation hit me. I cruised past the hospital.

Found the house without any trouble. A passing Franciscan glared at me, and I blamed the McDonald's bag. The last Franciscan I'd spoken to had been outside the abbey. Near Café Con Leche. I'd gone in to light a candle. As a child I'd learnt,

"A candle is a prayer in action."

Worked for me once.

The people I've loved most and treated the worst are all dead, buried in a cluster at Rahoon Cemetery. Visiting graves is a respected, honoured tradition in Ireland. I mean, do they have "Cemetery Sunday" in London?

I rest my case.

I am shocking in my duty. Rare and rarer do I go. Can't plead I meant better 'cause I didn't, then or now. So I sneak compensate. Thus the candles, like ready-made reparation. One of my favourite crime writers, Lawrence Block, has written fourteen Matt Scudder novels. The hero, a hopeless drunk in the early books, becomes a St Augustine–quoting, recovering alcoholic in the later ones. I like the early ones best. Matt, when he gets any cash, tithes his money. To any church, though the Catholics get the lion's share.

I'd put some money in the donations box and was standing outside when the friar appeared. A freezing cold day. I noticed his red toes in the open sandals. He said,

"Good for the circulation."

"I'm going to take your word on that."

Then, he'd given me the full stare. I learnt similar in the guards. It's not all intimidation, but it is related. He said,

"You're not from this parish."

"No, St Patrick's."

He frowned, definitely the lower end of the market, asked,

"And why are we blessed with your trade today?"

It crossed my mind to go,

"Fuck off."

But he was sockless, so I said,

"I was passing."

In my time, I've been barred from the best of pubs. Could only hope I wasn't going to add churches. The trick to priest-conversation is simple. Don't ever be surprised. They don't follow the usual rules. This guy was no exception, said,

"Do you know the two men I admire most?"

For a second, I thought he was going to launch into Don McLean's song that goes "The Father, Son and Holy Ghost". I tried to appear interested, asked,

"Who?"

"Charles Haughey and Eamonn Dunphy."

"Strange bedfellows. I'd have thought St Francis would have got a peek."

A car pulled up and he said,

"That's my taxi."

And he was gone.

All of this went through my mind as I rang Rita Monroe's bell.
The house was neat, tidy, respectable. Two storey with fresh net
curtains. From her laundry days, I thought. The door opened.
A tall, thin woman with steel-grey hair, tied in a severe bun. I
guessed her age at seventy, but she was very well preserved. An
almost unlined face. She retained traces of an impressive beauty.
Dressed all in white, she could have been a ward matron. She
asked,

"Yes?"

"Rita Monroe?"

"Yes."

"I'm Jack Taylor . . . I."

"Are you a guard?"

"Yes."

"Come in."

Led me into a sparse living room. Bare, except for the books,
thousands of them, neatly lined in every conceivable place. She
said,

"I like to read."

"Me, too."

Gave me an odd look, and I said,

"Guards do read."

She glanced at my brown paper bag, confused, asked,

"You brought your lunch?"

What the hell, I'd fly with the lie. Said,

"We have to grab a bite where we can."

I've never actually met a marine drill sergeant, but I can catch the drift. She had the eyes of one, said,

"I thought they'd send a uniform."

I had to pay attention. She thought I was a plainclothes. Decided to lean heavy on intuition, said,

"Mrs Monroe."

"Ms."

"I beg your pardon?"

"The correct form of address for a lady of unknown marital status is Ms."

As she said this, she appeared totally demented, and I nearly shouted,

"Spinster."

With my best interested, nay concerned, expression, I asked,

"Ms Monroe, would you like to tell me . . . in your own words . . . why you called us?"

Deep sigh. The only other woman on earth who could pull this shit so convincingly was my mother. Truth to tell, I was having difficulty seeing this person as "the angel of the Magdalen". Still, Bill had been adamant about her compassion. She said,

"This is the third time I've been broken into."

Then she paused, said,

"Shouldn't you be writing this down?"

Indeed.

I tapped my forehead, said,

"All goes in here."

No way was she buying that, so I prompted,

"Three occasions?"

"Yes, once in broad daylight."

She made a grimace of disgust, said,

"The most recent time . . . they relieved themselves on the carpets."

Feeling the pills coast, I nearly said,

"You're shitting me."

Went with,

"Very disturbing. Any idea of the culprits?"

She clicked her teeth. A disconcerting noise, almost related to "giddy-up". She said,

"From the estate no doubt."

"Ms Monroe, there are so many estates, could you be more specific?"

Now impatience showed and she snapped,

"Really! As if there could be any other."

"I see."

If she wasn't going to name it, then neither was I. I tried to appear thoughtful. As if I was weighing this.

I wasn't.

I said,

"I shall submit a full report."

She put her hands on her hips and smirked,

"In other words, you'll do nothing."

I stood up, thinking,

"The offer of tea would have helped."

She put her hand to her forehead, said,

"Oh."

And looked like she was going to faint. I steered her to a chair, got her sitting. She smelled of carbolic soap, like a harsh disinfectant. I asked,

"Can I get you something?"

"A little sherry. It's in the kitchen, the press above the kettle."

I went. The kitchen, too, was spotless. Demonically anti-septic. Found the sherry, got a water glass, poured a healthy measure, took a swig, thought,

"Jesus, that is sweet."

Took another. Yeah, almost treacle.

Bought the glass in. She took it in both hands, sipped daintily, said,

"I do apologise. I've recently had a bereavement."

If . . .

If I'd been paying attention, if I wasn't awash in chemicals, if I was more of a guard, if my head hadn't been up my arse . . .

I would have asked her about it. Maybe even heard the name and, oh God, what a ton of grief might have been averted.

Instead I asked,

"Are you OK?"

Her colour was returning. She said,

"You have been most kind."

The tone was alien to her. Gratitude did not come easily and certainly not naturally.

"Will you be all right? Should I call somebody?"

"No, no there's no one to call."

You hear that, you usually feel for the person. But I couldn't bring up that kind of feeling for her. If anything, she gave me a sense of revulsion. What I most wanted was to get the hell away from her. I blamed the sherry sloshing over the drugs, and that simply adds to my list of awful judgements. I said,

"I'll be off then."

Sounding like the Irish version of *Dixon of Dock Green*. She didn't speak as I let myself out. I'd been half tempted to nick a few of the books but didn't want to touch anything she owned.

As I walked down by the university, I could picture her, hunched in that chair, the lonely sherry beside her and not a sound in the house. A sense of triumph, at the very least a sense of relief of being now free of Bill Cassell, should have been happening.

It wasn't.

What I most focused on was the pint of Guinness I was going to have in about five minutes tops.

"Should I call Peter Mailer? I think not. Ever since he was cured of alcoholism he has acquired another compulsion. He stares deeply into your eyes and even the most trivial conversational opener provokes him into orgies of sincere nodding. I ascribe this to group therapy."

Nigel Williams, *Fortysomething*

The new day, mildly tranquillized, I crept into Nestor's. Jeff was on the phone, waved his hand. Was this . . . dismissal? . . . a barring order? . . . what? The sentry swirled his half empty glass, said,

"Second case of foot and mouth in the North."

"Right."

I didn't want to lean on it so added nothing. Jeff finished the call, said,

"Jack, what can I get you?"

Very worrying.

When you've fucked up big time and the fucker is being nice, search for a weapon. I said,

"Coffee's good."

"One coffee coming up."

It did.

He said,

"Grab a seat, I'll bring it over."

Ominous.

I sat, took out a virgin pack of reds, cranked up. Smoking as if I'd never stopped. Jeff came over, put the coffee down. As usual, he was wearing black jeans, boots and black waistcoat over long-sleeved granddad shirt. He asked,

"You hear about the young student?"

"Which one?"

"Who got capped on Eyre Square?"

"What about him?"

"The funeral's today."

"Oh."

"The reason I mention it is, we'll catch the overflow, and I know you don't do crowds too good."

"You got that right."

As I said, my head was up my ass. If I'd gone to the funeral, I'd have had all the answers.

I stood.

The speakers had kicked in and I'd vaguely registered a woman singing the blues. Not singing them as much as living them. I asked,

"Who's that?"

"Eva Cassidy, *The Fields of Gold* album."

"Ace, she ever comes to the Roisín, I'm there."

"I don't think so."

"You don't?"

"Cancer took her out. She was thirty-eight."

"Bummer."

I finished the coffee and headed off.

The sun was out and spring was knocking on heaven's door. A drinking school near the toilets, in chorus, shouted,

"Fucker."

Me?

Near the statue of Pádraic Ó Conaire, three teenage girls were sitting at the fountain. As usual, some wag had thrown colour into the water, and a technical kaleidoscope rose above their heads. They were singing,

"You make me whole again."

A number one for Atomic Kitten, at the top of the British charts.

The song finished and I joined the crowd in applause. A young girl tugged at my sleeve, hope bright in her eyes, asked,

"Are you Louis Walsh?"

"Me? No . . . sorry."

She looked devastated. I asked,

"Why'd you think I was?"

"You look old."

I could have simply rung Bill, said,

"I found her. She's at this address."

Did I? Did I fuck?

If I had, perhaps the whole show would have been wrapped there and then.

Or . . . unravelled.

But I had a burn for Bill. It was a long time since any emotion had fuelled me. I fed the hatred with playback of the gun barrel against my forehead. My hands would clench till the nails gouged into the palms. My teeth hurt from clenching them.

Man, it felt good.

Love or hate, go the distance with either, and whatever else, you are fucking electric. Crank it up a notch and sparks light your brain. Course I know, the brighter the glow, the more spectacular the crash. Nothing lights the sky like those shooting stars. Sat in my room, polished the Heckler & Koch. It is true: a weapon is the great equaliser. Is it ever?

In my head was Psalm 137. Boney M had a massive hit with part of it, back when the guards were my reason for being. In the psalm, the poet begs that he may be made happy by murdering the children of his enemies. Its music cries out with bloody restitution.

Course, if you're still familiar with Boney M, you are too far gone for any serious treatment.

It was ridiculously easy to find Bill's hired help, the guy who'd brought me to him and laughed at my degradation. I sat outside Sweeney's and simply clocked the times he came in and out. He was fixed in a routine. All I had to do now was decide when I'd take him. Nev would be another day's work. For him, I'd require time.

To celebrate the ease of this, I headed for a new pub, new to me at any rate, McSwiggan's in Wood Quay. Even sounds like a decent place.

A tree grows in Brooklyn.

And also in McSwiggan's.

Kidding I ain't. Smack in the back bar, a lovely solid tree. Only in Ireland. Don't cut the timber but do build the pub. I liked it already. Huge place. I settled near the tree.

Who wouldn't?

Had two sips dug in my Guinness when a woman approached. I thought,

"What a pub."

Then I clocked the neat tiny pearl earrings. Ban garda.

You don't have to be a policewoman to wear them, but ban gardaí have a certain style in their usage, that says,

"So OK, I'm a guard, but hey, I'm feminine, too."

Her age was in that blurred over thirty area that makeup can disguise. A pretty face, very dark hair and steel in her jaw line. She said,

"Jack Taylor."

Not a question, a statement. I said,

"Can I cop a plea?"

"May I sit down?"

"If you behave."

Glimmer of a smile. She said,

"I've heard about your mouth."

She spoke English like they do when they've been reared in the Gaeltacht. It is their second language. Never sits fully fluently. I said,

"Connemara?"

"Furbo."

"And you heard about my mouth . . . from . . . let's see . . . Superintendent Clancy?"

Frown, then shake of the head.

"No . . . others . . . but not him."

Her clothes were good but not great. Navy sweater with white collar, dark blue jeans and freshly white trainers. None of it designer gear, more Penney's than Gucci. They'd been given a lot of usage but were well maintained. Like her life, I surmised. She'd never rise above C-list status. She asked,

"How did you know I was a ban garda?"

"I used to be a guard."

Now she gave a dazzling smile, transformed her face. A mix of devilment and delight, the very best kind, said,

"Oh, I know that."

She was drinking something orange in a glass, with lots of ice. I'd bet heavy it was Britvic and nothing added. Here was your sensible girl. Drinking would be at weekends and never lethal. I asked,

"What do you want?"

"To talk."

My turn to smile, without devilment or even warmth, the one they teach you in Templemore. I asked,

"What about?"

She glanced over her shoulder, then I thought,

"What? Coke, pills, drink?"

"The Magdalen."

Caught me by surprise. I said,

"Oh."

"You're out of your depth. I can help."

I took a long swig of my pint, felt it massage my stomach.
I asked,

"And why would you want to do that?"

A moment, shadows flitted across her face, then,

"Because it's the right thing to do."

I drained my glass, asked,

"Get you something?"

"No, thank you."

"What's your name?"

"Bríd . . . Bríd Nic an Iomaire."

Had to digest that, reach into old memory for translation,
said,

"Ridge . . . am I right?"

She gave a disgusted look, said,

"We don't use the English form."

"Why does that not surprise me?"

I stood up, said,

"Hate to drink and run."

"You're going?"

"No wonder you're a policewoman."

"But don't you know that Superintendent Clancy's aunt was
a nun in the laundry?"

I tried not to show my surprise, and she said,

"See, you do need the guards."

"Honey, it's a long time since I needed anything from the guards."

"You're making a mistake."

"Believe me, it's what I do best."

"To her way of thinking, such mishaps were intimately connected to the intelligence of the recipient. Violence happened to people who, unlike her, did not have the common sense to avoid it."

Louise Doughty, *Honey Dew*

Two days later, I was drink free but drug ridden. The double dose of pills had me mellow beyond mantra. Spring was heavy in its promise, and despite a nip in the wind, people were in shirtsleeves. I was wearing a tie-dye T-shirt. Not by design but atrocious laundry. Women over the years had patiently explained the colours you never mix. Dutifully, I wrote the instructions down. Then washed the list.

So, a once splendidly white T had slugged it out against navy and . . . women forgive me . . . pink.

As in life, white lost.

Not a complete disaster as the logo had been near erased. Once it had read,

I WAS A GUARD.

NOW I'M A BLACKGUARD.

I was sitting on the rim of the fountain. To my right, was the statue of Pádraic Ó Conaire. His head was back. Yeah, he'd been decapitated, the stone whisked to Northern Ireland. Eventually, the culprits were caught, the piece returned.

If not the finest hour for the Guards, it remains among their most popular.

A drinking school was in full song near the public toilet. Sounded like "She Moved through the Fair", to the air of *Who Wants to Be a Millionaire.* Not an impossible task, simply weird. On Eyre Square, since the Celtic Tiger roared, weird was downright commonplace.

Add to it, the conglomerate of Italian, Spanish, Irish, American and, I swear, Serbo-Croat, you had lunacy on tap.

A woman detached herself from the pack, approached me, said,

"And a good morning to you, sir."

"Howyah?"

She was encouraged by my answer, moved closer. Her age could have been twenty-five or sixty from the ruined face and dead eyes. Her accent had the burr of Glasgow, which was no longer on her agenda. She asked,

"Price o' cup of tea, sir?"

"Sure."

Surprised her. When you surprise a wino, you have got a few moves left. I reached in my pocket, took out the change, handed it over. She took it fast. I asked,

"Ever hear of Pádraig?"

I meant the late head wino.

She glanced over at Pádraic Ó Conaire, asked,

"Who's he?"

"He wrote *M'Asal Bheag Dubh.*"

"He what?"

"Never mind."

"Got a smoke?"

"Sure."

I produced a pack of reds, shook the pack, and she grabbed

two, tore the filters off. A match from nowhere and she was en-
gulfed in smoke, asked,

"Are you a social worker?"

"Hardly."

"A guard?"

"Not any more."

"Want a ride?"

I laughed out loud. Blame the drugs.

I thought about Casey, Bill Cassell's muscle. The giant who had
delighted in my humiliation. The Sicilians say, if you're planning revenge, dig two graves. One for yourself.

As Melanie sang in the hopeful years,

"Yada, yada."

Or they say revenge is a dish best eaten cold. I was cold all
right.

A nun skipped by, trailing piety. If I asked her, she'd go for
company policy, incant "for it is in forgiving that we are forgiven".

I'd answer,

"Bollocks."

Stood up, stretched, felt almost light. I'd unwrap the gun,
polish the handle. I had Casey's routine down pat. It simply remained to take the next step.

Shoot him.

"Only a small crack . . . But cracks make caves collapse."

Aleksandr Solzhenitsyn

Nothing reflects those months of numbness, those months of almost coma, like my total selfishness. Foot and mouth came and went with barely a dent in my perception. I look back now and go,

"What the hell were you thinking?"

A British election was due on 7 June, and Tony Blair's tooth-ridden smile was everywhere. It registered zip on my radar. A time there'd been, I could have named the members of the houses of parliament and actually followed the House of Commons debate.

Now, I barely knew the Oireachtas. I did notice Des O'Malley had been canonised in a TV series. Haughey got blasted, but what was new in that? I caught a glimpse of him, shaken and frail, emerging from a car and the crowd chucking coins.

Coining it?

Not any more.

Louis Walsh had unveiled yet another global band on us. Girls this time. I had to know this as two were from Galway. How parochial had I become? Slowly, I was fading into my father. My mother continued her black ghost role around the streets. She haunted more than me.

Videos.

With my new chemical tranquillity, I was able to watch a whole slush of movies. In no particular order

> Loved
> Loathed
> Laughed
> Cried

Through

> *The Thin Blue Line*
> *The Company of Strangers*
> *Audition*
> *Jennifer Eight*
> *Smiley's People*
> *Sunset Boulevard*

Listened to Gabrielle; listened to her a lot. *Sunshine* seemed to speak to me, but I'm not sure what it tried to tell me.

Books:

> *Robbers,* Christopher Cook
> *Noise Abatement,* Carol Ann Davis
> *1980,* David Peace

You bundle all that up, take it to a shrink, spill it on his desk and ask,

"What?"

He reaches for the Thorazine.

A snap analysis is given by any wino:

"You're seriously fucked."

Argue that.

As a footnote to the above, I was scrabbling through old photos when I found a battered leather purse, the type to hold a rosary beads. Opened it to reveal . . . my wedding ring.

Back from the Thames?

It's not that I survived that period. More along the lines of the Doors' biography:

No One Here Gets Out Alive.

Felt I wasn't hurting as the scar tissue encircled my soul, waiting to squeeze.

The day of the suicide began slow and easy. Woke in a sub-dued mood, not unpleasant. More in the neighbourhood of gentle melancholia than chemical overload.

I could hack that.

Did some sit-ups and then had a cold shower. Who needed booze?

Not I.

Welcome to the world of pill dependency. When that kick-back came, as come it would, I figured to put a bullet in my head. No more hospitals or dry outs. Ride the dragon to the close.

Brewed some coffee and could actually taste it. Tasted good. I had a longing but didn't know for what.

God? Naw, He folded His tent and moved east. How much would I notice?

In the lobby of the hotel, Mrs Bailey exclaimed,

"Gosh, Mr Taylor, you look so relaxed!"

You betcha.

Even accepted her invitation to breakfast. Now that is a rib broke in the devil.

The chambermaid, housekeeper, cleaner, Janet, was also the waitress, albeit a slow one. I strongly suspected she might also be the cook. The breakfast lounge was bright and cheerful, a stack of gratis newspapers at the entrance. Mrs Bailey saw me glance at them, said,

"Oh, yes, just like the grand hotels. You can have the *Independent* or . . . the *Independent!*"

And she gave a mischievous smile. A pure joy to behold. She liked to nail her politics up front. We sat and she said,

"Janet irons them."

"What?"

"Every morning, every newspaper. So the guests don't get ink on their hands."

I'd seen Anthony Hopkins do it in *Remains of the Day* but put it down to an English foible. We ordered tea, toast and scrambled eggs. Mrs Bailey said,

"Smoke if you must."

I didn't.

I felt relaxed, touching mellow. Remember Donovan? If he was the English answer to Bob Dylan, you shudder to think what the question was. He wore the denim cap, had the face of a pixie, and I could remember "Atlantis".

God help me.

Lived in North Cork now and, like the other expat rock stars, liked to jam in his local pub. His daughter was the actress Ione Skye. And before the eggs arrive, I was asking myself,

"How do I know this shit?"

And worse, why?

Mrs Bailey touched my arm. I noticed the glut of liver spots on her hand. She asked,

"Where were you?"

"In the sixties."

A shot of sadness in her eyes, and she said,

"You live there a lot."

"In the sixties?"

"The past."

I nodded, accepting the truth of it, said,

"It's not that it's safer, but I dunno, familiar."

A huge pot of tea came, and she opened the lid, stirred vigorously, said,

"I never got used to tea bags."

A man stopped, said,

"Did ye hear?"

In Ireland this could mean the pope is dead or it's stopped raining. We gave the requisite,

"What happened?"

"The FAI Cup . . . Bohs beat Longford Town."

I'd have been more torn up if I knew Longford were even playing. Mrs Bailey, who watched all sport, said,

"That dote Michael Owen had two miraculous goals on Saturday, finished Arsenal."

A woman over eighty, in the west of Ireland, knew that, and I wasn't even sure what day of the week it was. The man, crushed, lamented,

"The dream is over for Longford."

And he sloped away, defeat writ large. I said,

"A Longford man."

"Ary, go away, he's from Tuam."

Brendan Flood was on my mind. Time for another meet. Now that he'd lost his religion and hit the booze, I felt I should check on him. We weren't friends, but we were connected. His information had broken two cases for me. Found his number, rang,

To my surprise, a woman answered. I said,

"Could I speak to Brendan please?"

Keep it low and keep it polite.

"Who is this?"

"Jack Taylor . . . I'm a friend of Brendan's."

Long pause, then,

"Ye were guards together."

I took a moment, considered, then,

"Yeah, a long time ago."

"Not for Brendan. He was always a guard."

"Um, could I speak to him?"

"No."

Like a slap in the mouth. I regrouped, tried,

"Excuse me?"

"He hung himself."

"To this scene come Eddie and Ray Bob, outsiders from the rural frontier, from the unseen and forgotten bumfuck outskirts of the urban media landscape. Rubbernecking the city, seeing what's what, not much impressed. Just more folks humping the dollar."

Christopher Cook, *Robbers*

Brendan Flood had left an envelope addressed to
"*Jack Taylor.*"

I offered to come round, she said,

"I don't want you in my house."

Fair enough.

Anyone who thinks suicide is an easy option might reconsider, especially if a rope is their choice, Brendan had put the noose around a sturdy beam, then, dressed in his guard uniform, climbed on to a plain kitchen chair. A guy in Bohermore used to handcraft them. Built to last. The rope near decapitated him. He'd vented his bowels, ruining the trousers. I was given all these details by the young guard who'd had to cut him down.

I asked Mrs Flood,

"When is the funeral?"

"From Flaherty's, at six tomorrow . . . to St Patrick's. He'll be buried in the new cemetery."

"Can I do anything?"

"Leave me alone."

Click.

I could not believe he was dead. That I'd failed him was obvious. Remembered all the shit I'd read about "Gatekeepers", how it said,

Gatekeepers are the first people to realise the potential suicide is serious. They are the first "finder". It's their duty, responsibility, to direct the potential suicide towards help.

Oh God . . . finder! My whole career now was based on a rep as finder. And gatekeeper! Could there be a worse example than me. I'd flung the frigging gate wide open, had as good as said,

"Go hang yourself."

The pure legacy of suicide is the survivors' guilt. A barrage of questions that can never be answered:

Could I have helped?

Why didn't I act?

How blind was I?

All now useless. I wanted to crawl into a whiskey cloud and never emerge. Personify *The Cloud of Unknowing*.

Guilt roared up my body to emerge as a howl of total anguish. Oh Christ, yet another grave to join the long line that I so badly neglected.

Dry swallowed some Quaaludes in the hope of artificial peace. They'd need to be mothers. Lay on the bed, sobbed intermittently. As the pills kicked in, my eyes began to close. My last thought,

"Hope they frigging kill me."

They didn't.

But did they ever knock me out. Came to in darkness. Checked my watch, 8.30 p.m. Jesus. And knew what I was going to do.

Dressed in black, not least for Brendan. Jeans, T-shirt, watch cap. Fitted the gun into the waistband of my jeans. Checked myself in the mirror. The face reflected was a chunk of worn granite. When your eyes look hard to yourself, you've gone west.

Made a caffeine-loaded drink, washed down some black beauties. Took deep breaths, said,

"Incoming."

The docks were quiet. Less than a tourist away was Eyre Square with its attendant madness. Wouldn't you know, caught on the wind was David Gray's "This Year's Love".

Slaughters me. I can sing every lyric and, worse, mean it. Tear the goddamn heart right out.

I'd roared at the sky,

"God, why torment me so?"

Course He didn't answer. Least not in any fashion I could decipher. Even Thomas Merton couldn't help me there.

As I neared Sweeney's, I could feel the gun butt, cold against my skin. My mind was closing down on all fronts. Could have been the drugs . . . or grief. I'd never understood the connections it makes at such times of intensity. In rehab, on one of my numerous incarcerations, a shrink had said,

"Your mental processes suggest an underlying psychosis. It's significant that in periods of stress, you fix on passages from books you've read."

He'd rambled on in a pseudo-American style, using the term empathy a lot.

They do that, watch your wallet; it's going to cost.

Now a piece from Pete Hamill's *Why Sinatra Matters* surfaced.

Italians had suffered in their adopted America. In New Orleans, a jury had acquitted eight Italians on murder charges, reached no

verdict on a further three. Citizens went ape, claimed it was a mafia fix. A mob of several thousand stormed the jail. Two Italians were hanged screaming from lampposts. Another was shot with hundreds of bullets. Seven were executed by firing squads. Two more had crawled into a doghouse, were found and butchered.

In his sixties, Frank Sinatra said,

When I was young, people used to ask me why I sent money to the NAACP. I used to say, because we've been there too, man. It wasn't just black people hanging from the end of those fucking ropes.

Amen.

A tiny alley is a few doors up from Sweeney's. Even in daylight, it's dark. For a brief time, a drinking school set up there till the blackness ran them off. Winos more than most people seek the light. I got in there, checked my watch . . . 10.30 p.m. If Casey were as habitual as I'd observed, he'd be swinging by in an hour. Hunkered down against the wall, got almost comfortable. A rat shot out from the wall, scampered over my legs and was gone. I hadn't moved. You never want to focus their attention. A chill ran along my legs from where he'd touched. You have water, you have rats, don't sweat it, but I did.

Who wouldn't?

Took out the piece, examined it by touch.

Knew the details by rote:

> Heckler & Koch, H-K-4 double action pistol
> .32-calibre, 8-shot magazine
> Barrel: 3/50
> Weight: 16 oz

Stock: black plastic

Sights: fixed blade front

Features: gun comes with all parts prepared.

What more could you need to know?

One of the very best handguns on the market.

If you ever want to bore a woman rigid, list the above.

If you can't impress your mates with football, list the above.

Vive la différence.

Heard the sounds of the bar closing. People on the street, shouts and laughter, a guy came into the alley, and I crouched lower. He unzipped and let loose a volley.

I thought,

"You pig, you couldn't use the pub toilet?"

Nearly shot him.

He gave a sigh of relief, buttoned up and headed off. I wanted to roar,

"Wash your hands."

Things quietened down. The docks have never been a place to linger. You move fast. All the gentrification, all the prosperity, wouldn't change that. Stall here you'd get nailed. I moved to the front of the alley, holding the HK down along my right leg. Took some deep breaths. Heard a loud

"Goodnight."

Then the pub door pulled shut.

Here he was, the bold Casey. Lumbering by in the white tracksuit. I raised the gun, fired twice into the back of his right knee. The Belfast special. I moved, turned left, walked rapidly towards the Victoria Hotel. Two minutes.

In three, I was among the crowds jostling for the nightclub. Tore the cap off, opened my jacket.

Four, I was through the doors of the Great Southern, nodding at the porter. He said,

"Jack."

"How yah doing?"

Six, I caught the last order from a young barman.

"Large Jameson, pint of Guinness."

And I sunk into those embracing couches at the end of the foyer, a bust of James Joyce on a shelf above. I raised the pint, sank a level, then the whiskey, a mouthful, tilted the glass upwards, said,

"Here's looking at you, Jimmy."

Now, I thought, I just have to find Nev, the one who'd played the Russian roulette, and I'd have something medieval for him.

In 1985, we had the summer of moving statues. All over the country, the statues were on the move. I was stationed at Mount Mellary in Waterford, and for nine nights, the Virgin appeared to three children. I was assigned crowd control, and I was too pissed to control a match. The very air was full of expectation as each night the people gathered to see the Virgin. By then, my cynicism had kicked in full time and I asked my sergeant,

"So, if the crowd get excited, am I to use the baton on them?"

He gave me the look, sighed and said,

"In a country where statues walk and children speak directly to Our Lady, do you seriously think a baton is going to make the slightest difference?"

All I'd learned in the intervening years was that if you wanted to make a difference, a gun sure tipped the balance. The statues had long since ceased to move, but the country had gone to the dogs. The message from the visionaries had been that Ireland would be saved! The Celtic Tiger gave the lie to that. I picked up a book. This train of thought had sparked a memory, and I found the passage that went like this:

"But I'd still bet none of the pimply neighbours and second cousins on your list ever came upstairs with a twenty-five-cal semi auto. Is that fun?"

"No," she says, "a gun takes the fun out of fucking."

From *Hollowpoint* by Bob Reuland.

Next morning, I pilled ahead of the hangover. Cut it off at the pass. Brendan's funeral, I'd have to look half right. Went to the abbey, asked for a mass card. The guy there looked about a hundred. And to judge by his manner, none of them easy years. He barked,

"Name of deceased?"

"Brendan Flood."

"Single or series?"

"What?"

"One mass or a whole bunch?"

I tried to appear as if I was seriously contemplating this, then,

"Single, I guess."

Was going to add,

"With salt and vinegar."

But let it slide.

His expression said,

"Cheap bastard."

I asked,

"How much is that in Euro?"

It was a lot. I was tempted to say,

"Couldn't I just rent a mass?"

But he was already shutting the grille, and I barely slipped in,

"God bless."

Next to order a wreath. Went to the same florist, same girl
I'd been to so many times. She gave me a huge smile, said,

" 'Tis yourself."

You have to be Irish to catch the full flavour of that. Then,

"Is it wedding or funeral?"

I let her see my face, work it out. She did.

"Oh, I am sorry."

"Me, too."

"Something simple or decorative?"

"Something expensive."

She gave me the saddest smile. We knew. The banner riding
front, guilt riding shotgun. I gave her the details and she asked,

"A message?"

"Yes, 'To the Last Guard'."

A Galway girl, she had the class not to ask the meaning. I'm
not altogether sure I could have explained anyway. When I was
going, she said,

"You're a good man."

"Don't I wish?"

Saw the crowds as I neared the funeral home. Had to fight to
view the remains. Relatives were lined inside the door. I put
the mass card in the basket, joined the queue to file past Brendan. An open casket.

Fuck.

He looked like a wax effigy. His neck, of course, was covered
with a high collar. Despite the undertakers' best efforts, they
couldn't disguise the grimace of his mouth. If you've been almost beheaded, smiling you weren't. What scarred me the most
was a bruise on the bridge of his nose. Deep and . . . sore, oh
God.

His hands were folded on his chest, a rosary beads interwoven through the fingers. Like handcuffs. I wanted to touch his hand, but the coldness would freak me. I'd lose it entirely, muttered,

"Goodbye, buddy."

Lame . . . and don't I know that.

Shook hands with a gaggle of relatives. I said,

"So sorry."

They intoned,

"Thank you for your trouble."

Murder.

A brief blessing and a decade of the rosary before the priest dismissed us. Outside, the men produced packs of

Carroll's

Major

and

Silk Cut Ultra's.

Leaning against the wall, in civvies, was Superintendent Clancy, his finger up, beckoning me. He'd dropped a few pounds; he sure needed to. I clocked two burly minders a few yards away. Serious protection.

I strolled over, said,

"Super."

"Jack, good to see you."

The bonhomie was worrying. A time we'd been friends. Oh . . . so very long ago. I said,

"Been to Weight Watchers, eh?"

"Stress, laddie . . . that and golf."

"Good of you to show for Brendan."

I half meant it.

Clancy looked round, as if fearful he'd be overhead, said,

"He could have been a great one, real nose for investigation, but he got religion."

He made it sound like a disease, paused, then,

"Like you, Jack, except the bottle got your arse."

I could have let it slide but for Brendan. Some effort was necessary. I said,

"Gee, either of us might have climbed the ladder and got . . . what? . . . golf . . . and fat?"

He signalled to his minder, brushed lint off his lapel, said,

"Guy got shot last night."

"Yeah?"

"A runner for your old mate, that piece of work, Bill Cassell."

"You'll no doubt be conducting a thorough investigation."

He looked me right in the eye, said,

"I won't lift a bloody finger."

He smirked, turned to the minder, snapped,

"What are you standing there for? Get the bloody car."

My turn to smile, said,

"Authority you wear like a loose garment."

Stomped off.

I noticed Bríd Nic an Iomaire among the mourners; she must have been on duty and arrived late. She looked devastated. I figured it was her first guard death. Even if he was an ex-guard, you are never really out of the loop.

I thought I'd go over to her, but she had moved away.

"appreciate what I might read was nearly . . . oh so very nearly left unread, the litter of a mangled mind."

K.B.

Fr Malachy, as always the presiding priest, was lighting one Major from the butt of another. I said,

"Nice service."

"Ah, there's little you can say about a suicide, little that's any good anyway."

Through a cloud of smoke, he glared, said,

"They're well rid of him."

"Wow, you bleed with compassion."

Then his expression changed, a sly glint to his eyes. There's few more chilling than a sly priest. It's all that theological back-up as weight. He said,

"When I heard an ex-guard topped himself, I thought it was you. Would have laid odds on it."

"And break my poor mother's heart?"

He waved me away, but I wasn't done, asked,

"You still getting 'contributions' from her then?"

He went pale, had to physically rein in, said,

"You'd like a good puck, wouldn't you?"

"That is a 'P', isn't it. Unless it's a whole other deal."

Before he went coronary, a woman approached, said,

"Jack Taylor?"

I turned . . . Mrs Flood, in the black mourning gear, like a withered jackdaw. I said,

"So sorry for your loss."

"He's no loss. Here."

Shoved an envelope at me. Brendan's note. I didn't know what to say. She said,

"Oh don't worry, I didn't open it."

"I didn't think you would."

"Yes, you did. You might not wear the uniform but you're still a guard. God blast ye."

She hadn't spit on me, but I wiped my face as if she had, muttered,

"Enough."

Walked towards Forster Street. Walked fast.

THE MAGDALEN

The laundry was doing great business, to such an extent that locals began dropping in their clothes. No compassion from them. The girls had chalk complexions, and as they rarely left the building, they resembled the starched sheets they were cleaning. The lack of sunlight and the stifling conditions added to the look of utter hopelessness the girls shared. Known as penitents, they were expected to say the rosary as they worked. Visiting clergy reminded them of their fall from grace and how far they'd have to climb if redemption was ever to be achieved.

Lucifer entered the laundry each time with an almost dizzying sense of power. Her eyes had become accustomed to the harsh emanations from the soap, bleach, steam and constant boiling water. The smell of perspiration and the stench of unwashed bodies only served to stoke her simmering rage. She hated these girls for reasons even she couldn't understand.

Next day, before the funeral, I rang Bill Cassell. He barked,

"What do you want, Taylor?"

"Gee, Bill, what happened to Jack?"

"Don't fuck with me today, fellah."

"I found the woman."

Intake of breath, then,

"Where?"

"Newcastle."

"Tell me about it."

I did.

He was silent as he digested the data. I said,

"So, we're quits . . . right?"

"What?"

"You said I could wipe the slate if I found her."

"Yeah, yeah, you're clear."

I could have left it, but I wanted to needle the fuck, said,

"You don't sound so good, Bill."

"Casey got shot."

Push a tad further, asked,

"Who's Casey?"

Low mean chuckle and,

"Surprised you've forgotten him. Big guy in a white track-suit, held you during our last little chat. Course you never got to see Nev, and if you're lucky, you never will."

"Oh."

"Yeah, some cowardly shite kneecapped him."

"That's gotta hurt."

"Like you care."

"Any idea who did it?"

"Well, I can safely rule you out."

"Why?"

"Two reasons. One, you're usually too pissed to aim your dick, and two, you haven't the balls."

Click.

Hard to say if I'd scored on that exchange. I was wearing the dark suit again, conscious that today Brendan Flood would be six foot under. His letter was beside my bed. I hadn't yet been able to open it. Dropped two 'ludes and made some coffee. Turned the radio on. Bob Dylan was sixty.

Finally got the Oscar for his song in *Wonder Boys*.

They played it, "Things Have Changed".

Had they ever.

As the English say, and changed "irrevocably".

Good word, makes you feel educated. Best to use it sparingly. I would.

Checked my watch, realised the 'ludes had kicked as I'd forgotten to drink the coffee.

Lit a cigarette.

Took a breath, opened the envelope, my mind going,

"And the winner is . . ."

It began:

Jack,

What can I tell you? I ran out of energy. When I ran out of faith, it was all over bar the shouting. No doubt you'll hear the shouting at my funeral. That Magdalen business was just the final straw. Clancy and his crowd are keen to keep it in the past. As if evil can be ever put in the bin. That Bill Cassell doesn't want to find the woman for any good reason. Watch him and your step. My wife gets the house and money. But us guards, we keep some in reserve. Go to AIB, Lynch's Castle, Savings Account number 19426421, and you'll get the land of your life. I'd have stayed longer if the hangovers were less tolerable. I don't even mean the ones from booze. You're the closest I ever had to a friend, and I'm not even sure I liked you. So, I've been dead longer than I thought. If I believed in God any more, I'd say, God bless you.

I wish I could have been the guard you could have been.

Slán.

Brendan Flood

I folded the letter carefully, put it in my wallet. Beside the photo of the girl with the brown ringlets, a relic of Padre Pio was riding back up. The Irish word for sadness is *brónach*. But it means so much more than that. It's akin to desolation, and my heart was shot through with it.

In the lobby, Mrs Bailey asked,

"Breakfast?"

"No, thank you."

"Are you all right? You look shook."

"I've to go to a funeral."

"Somebody close?"

"I think so."

"I'll say a prayer for him."

"Thank you."

After the funeral mass, I elected to walk behind the hearse. A custom that's fading, I need it like confession. Still, despite rampant commercialism, passers-by stopped, took off caps, blessed themselves. That touches me in a way that religion never has. Walking, too, was a sprinkle of guards. Not in uniform but present. As always, they gave me the cautious nod, Bríd Nic an Iomaire among them. I am of . . . but not among them.

I was one of the men who helped hold the ropes that lower the casket into the hole. God, it was heavy. We lost it a bit towards the end, and the coffin hit the dirt with a sound like "AH".

Like the gentlest sigh escaping

Fr Malachy intoned,

"Man, who has but a short time to live, is full of misery."

I hate that piece. As if things weren't bad enough. After, he made a beeline for me, but I wasn't in the mood for the ejit, said,

"Piss off."

I saw the gravediggers smile.

For that alone, it was worth it.

In the Celtic tradition, there was the beautiful notion of *"anam cara"; anam* is the Irish word for soul and *cara* is the word for friend. In the *anam cara,* friendship, you are joined in an ancient way with the friend of your soul. So wrote John O'Donohue in his book, *Eternal Echoes.*

For too long I'd been neglecting Jeff and Cathy. Told myself,

" 'Cause, they have a new baby, give them space."

I half believed this shit sometimes. The old saying,

"If you have to know any act, let it be your own."

Whoops.

Wore a sweatshirt that read:

667

(NEIGHBOUR OF THE BEAST)

And the faded 501s.

Then remembered the AIB. Got out the account number, checked it and memorised it. Mrs Bailey was reading the *Irish Independent,* said,

"Do you know who's dead?"

It doesn't get more Irish.

I said,

"I already know who's dead, believe me."

She gave me a head on look, said,

"That's a very relaxed outfit."

"I'm a relaxed kind of guy."

She gave a polite smile, with,

"Not a description I'd have applied myself."

Went to the bank first. A non-national was perched on a mat outside, asked,

"Euro please."

"Gimme a minute, all right?"

"One minute, I am counting."

The temptation to crack his skull rose with the rejoinder,

"Count on that."

Make local headlines with

EX-GARDA ATTACKS REFUGEE.

And they would.

Into the bank and presented my account number to a cashier. She had the moneyed face, hard, hard, hard.

A nametag proclaimed "Siobhan".

She tapped in the numbers, said,

"This account has been opened for Jack Taylor."

I gave her the refugee smile, said,

"I am he."

No brownie points. She frosted,

"I'll need to see some ID."

I'd been expecting this, plonked the following down: passport, driver's licence, library card.

She examined them like a tax inspector, snapped,

"This licence has expired."

"A metaphor for my life."

She looked up, obviously not happy with my appearance. I said,

"Siobhan, lighten up, this isn't a tribunal."

"There is a considerable sum here."

"No shit?"

Came involuntarily, but who could fault me? She stood up, said,

"I'll have to consult a manager."

"Gee, that's surprising."

Eventually a suit approaches, says,

"Mr Taylor, welcome to the AIB."

I'm wondering how much is a considerable sum?

And asked exactly that.

He looks round, says,

"You can have a printout of the balance."

"Well, let's have it."

When I get it, I didn't look, shoved it in my pocket, said,

"Tell Siobhan I love her."

Came out to find the guards arresting the refugee. I, like the horseman, passed by.

"Be selfish, stupid and have good health.
But if stupidity is lacking, then all is lost."

Flaubert's dictum for getting through life unscathed

Into Garavan's, shouted a pint and took a seat in the snug.

Snug it is.

The pint came, I took a belt, pulled out the statement, shouted,

"Brandy, large."

And punched the air. It wasn't retirement money, but for some time to come, I wouldn't be counting the shillings. Not with any caution anyway. When the brandy came, the guy asked,

"Celebrating?"

"I am. What will you have?"

"A decade of the rosary."

You can never impress them in that bar. I wanted to sit there all day, but my conscience whined,

"Yo, what about Jeff and Cathy?"

So I went to Nestor's. The sentry was in place, his half before him. Jeff was washing glasses. The sentry said,

"Didn't you used to drink here?"

Jeff smiled.

I climbed on a stool, said,

"Sorry I've been out of touch."

"Good to see you, Jack."

"How's Cathy?"

"Good."

"And the baby?"

Blame the brandy, I couldn't remember the baby's name. Mortified, I fumbled for my cigs, cranked up as Jeff said,

"She's thriving."

And the conversation died. Didn't splutter to a slow stop or meander some clichéd route and collapse. I said, after a horrendous amount of time,

"A pint, Jeff."

"Coming up."

Got that and moved to what used to be my office. Hard chair and table, with my back to the door, thinking,

"Finish the pint and flee."

Jeff came over, mug of coffee in his hand, asked,

"Join you?"

"Sure."

He did.

Then asked,

"Where are you on Bob Dylan?"

"In the dark mostly."

Head shake, wrong answer.

He launches.

"Look back for a moment to *Don't Look Back,* the documentary film of his '65 visit to Britain, when he was young and beautiful. Here he is, just turning twenty-four, with the world of celebrity and glamour kissing his feet. He is the most perfectly hip creature on earth."

Jeff pauses, caught in the sheer wonder of this image. Shakes his head, continues,

"Imagine how you would cope with this. Even 10 per cent of it would turn your head. But Dylan does cope, telling the man from *Time* magazine, 'You're going to die. You're going to be dead. It could be twenty years; it could be tomorrow, anytime. So am I. I mean we're just going to be gone. The world's going to go on without us, you do your job in the face of that, and how seriously you take yourself, you decide.'

"This is the Dylan stance. Thirty-six years on, he's still all alone in the end-zone, determinedly unimpressed by the hullabaloo he has engendered and endured throughout."

Jeff took a swipe of his coffee, beads of sweat on his brow. Mr Cool, Mr Mellow, Mr Laid back had got passion. Before I could say that, he said,

"That's not my rap; it's from a piece by Michael Gray, a Dylan chronicler from way back."

"And what? You learnt it by heart?"

He caught my tone, defended,

"What if I did?"

"Come on, Jeff, you were a musician, nigh on Dylan's era. You've survived, too."

The bar radio kicked in, and the Kinks' "Lola" began. We both smiled. Perhaps it was the last comment on us.

Like asking,

"Riddle me this?"

I said,

"Did you read Ray Davies' book?"

"What, you don't think I've enough grief."

I'd finished the pint and was debating another when he said,

"Do you know what it's like to have a Down's syndrome child?"

I'd no idea, said,

"I've no idea."

"Would you like to know?"

Before I could answer, he reached in his jeans, took out a folded paper, said,

"That will tell you."

"Did you write it?"

"No, I live it."

Then he was up, said,

"I've a beer delivery. They'll throw the barrels all over the yard unless I'm there."

I opened the paper, read

Welcome to Holland
By Emily Pearl.

It was a long piece about planning a trip to Italy. Goes into lengthy detail about the excitement of the trip. This is the one you've planned all your life. You've even learnt the language and have all the sights outlined that you've always wanted to see. But when the plane lands, you're in Holland; and bewildered, you ask how this can happen? All your arrangements are geared for Italy. After the initial shock has worn off, you begin to slowly see the wonders of Holland, different though they are from everything you had anticipated. You have to learn the new language and change all the expectations to adapt to this new landscape. Gradually, you begin to enjoy the benefits of Holland, though it takes a huge shift of perspective. In time, you actually come to love Holland, the last thing you'd have believed.

I sat there, my heart in ribbons. I no longer wanted that

drink. One way or another, I felt, I too had been mourning Italy all my life.

I did the only thing I could. I went out and bought a bunch of tulips for Cathy.

*"The thirst for knowledge is like a piece of ass you know
you shouldn't chase; in the end, you chase it just the same."*

George P. Pelecanos, *Down by the River Where the Dead Men Go*

Friday evening, a young man came out of his FÁS course. He
was doing well. He had a few bob in his pocket and was meeting the lads in Cuba.

The club, not the country.

A buzz was in the air, with all the false promise of the weekend. He stood for a minute at the back of the cathedral. Course, being the sparkling new generation, it never occurred to him to bless himself. Why would he? That ritual was rare to rarer. Who needs God at seventeen?

On a whim, he crossed over to the embankment, down the steps to where the ducks are. He stood at the edge, feeling good. Never heard the man. People use that path from the old mill up to the bridge regularly. It's a snatch of tranquillity from the hectic Newcastle Road.

The man stopped, put two bullets in the young lad's head, turned and went back towards the mill. If the splash of the body was loud, it didn't cause him to look back. He flicked the empty wrapper from the gum into the river.

Witnesses, yet again, would provide a maelstrom of conflicting information. I heard about it in Nestor's. Jeff said,

"God almighty, what's with the world?"

The sentry said,

"I blame the tribunals."

Before I could comment, the door opened and Terry Boyle came storming in. The blond hair awry, his tall frame rigid with anger, he was wearing a very good suit. Towered over me, shouted,

"What the hell am I paying you for?"

I was at my regular table, a book before me. I used my index finger to indicate the other hard chair. He said,

"Don't tell me what to do."

"Sit down or I'll knock you down."

For a moment, I could see the veins throb at his temples. Weighing the odds. Jeff had tensed, and Terry glanced round, sized him up, then snapped,

"Barkeep, a vodka tonic and make it soon."

He sat.

I noticed lesions on the tips of his fingers. Tried to recall anything I'd learned in my Templemore days. He had said he was in software, so I said,

"Those from typing."

The sneer turned his mouth ugly, and he near spat his reply,

"Jesus, you old guys. Nobody types any more; it's called keying."

I leant near, said,

"Come here."

Startled look and,

"What?"

"Come on, move closer."

He didn't, so I said,

"You shout at me again, and I mean ever, I'll put your balls out through your throat . . . key that."

He straightened his back, said,

"I practise Kai-tai-wan."

Least I think that's what he said. Before I could respond, Jeff plonked his drink on the table, said,

"Sonny, you burst into my pub like a lunatic again, you'll need that Kai whatever."

And was gone.

Terry let out his breath, whined,

"What's with you old guys? You're so goddamn touchy."

The lapse into American didn't endear, but I let it slide, got my smokes out, and fired up. He said,

"Haven't you heard of the patches?"

"Terry, take a moment, have your drink, and we'll start over. How would that be?"

He did.

I said,

"What's the bug up your arse?"

"I haven't received a single progress report. How are you spending my money? Kirsten is spending money like a drunken sailor. My father's money."

Truth to tell, I'd all but forgotten the whole deal, said,

"I'm working on a definite line of inquiry."

Stopped myself from adding

"An arrest is imminent."

He eyed me with huge disbelief, said,

"You're on to something?"

"Am I ever?"

He took a sip of the vodka, grimaced, said,

"And you can drink . . . what . . . like every day?"

"It's my duty."

He let that go, rubbed his hands, said,

"OK, this is very promising. You think the bitch will go down?"

I nodded solemnly.

He reached in his jacket, his very expensive jacket, took out his chequebook, said,

"A further two weeks' retainer sufficient to nail the cunt?"

I nearly gasped. The word hits me like a gossip in heat. Felt my fists clench but went for economic damage, said,

"To wrap it clean, let's say a month."

He wrote the cheque. I noticed the pen, a beautiful piece of work. I was schooled the old way. Hammered knuckles over wooden desks to perfect our penmanship. We got stinging fingers but legible handwriting. About as useful as a reference from Fianna Fáil. He caught the stare, said,

"It's a Mont Blanc, the Agatha Christie limited edition. Want to hold it?"

"I don't know? I might not want to give it back."

He offered. Felt the weight immediately, examined it slow. True artistry, made me long for things I didn't need. He took it back, said,

"Out of your league, Pops."

"Terence, you're really going to have to mind your language."

His expression now was rampant with the New Ireland, smug, greedy, knowing. He said,

"I have a set of these, cost more than you'd earn in your whole miserable life."

I decided he was too stupid for a slap in the mouth. I could wait. Jeff moved out from the bar, began to sweep the floor. I had never seen him do that. Terry didn't notice; the hired help was of no consequence. He said,

"Are you free tonight?"

"You're what? Asking me for a date?"

He gave a small titter. I wish I could call it a laugh, even settle for its relation, the giggle . . . but no . . . it was rough. He said,

"Geraldo and I are holding a soirée in my pad."

"Pad! And who's Geraldo?"

He gave the first real smile I'd seen, said,

"My significant other. It's our anniversary."

I lit another cig, drew deep. He continued,

"We've been an item for twelve months."

"And this, it's for gays only I suppose."

"Ah, Jack . . . you don't mind if I call you that? . . . we have friends in every walk of life."

"And you want me to come . . . why? Bit of rough trade?"

"Don't be so hard on yourself, Jack. You have a certain primitive allure. My address is on the card I gave you. It'll be a fun thing."

Then he was up, saying,

"Eight-thirty onwards, dress seventies."

"I thought I already did."

At the door, he collided with the sweeping Jeff. Neither apologised. He moved to Jeff's right and was gone. A few minutes later, Jeff started back for the counter, dropped something on my table. The Mont Blanc.

I said,

"Jeez, Jeff."

"Teach him some manners."

"But you're a musician; where did you learn that stunt?"

"It's called improvisation. Wouldn't be much of an artist without that."

"He'll know . . . Jeff, he'll know you took it."

"I'm seriously hoping you're right."

*"She had a stuffed animal collection. I was pretty sure. Her Corolla
had either a smiley face or a Jesus fish affixed to the bumper. She read
John Grisham novels, listened to soft rock, loved going to bridal showers
and had never seen a Spike Lee movie."*

Dennis Lehane, *Prayers for Rain*

As best as I could, I avoided the Claddagh. Not that I disliked
the area. On the contrary, it used to be part of my heritage. The
whole deal: feed the swans, walk to Grattan Road, make wishes
from the end of Nimmo's Pier.

But it sure held bad karma.

These days, now that the depression was in chemical abeyance,
I was suffused with memory. Veered from the bitter-sweet to
crucifixion. Did books save my sanity? You bet your ass.

On any given day, I'd have a volume in my jacket, read, read,
read.

As if I meant it.

Most times I did.

Walking down Quay Street, now being touted as the Temple
Bar of Galway, I noticed the remnants of the English stag parties. Truly a blight on any landscape. The street ablaze with
coffee shops, pizzerias, bistros, all staffed with non-Irish. You'd
be lucky to hear English, never mind a hint of a brogue. Holding some sort of anchor was McDonagh's, the place for fish
and chips. Always packed. Get a hint of sun and people would
be sprawled as far as Jury's. If I want real fish and chips, I go to

Conlon's, handily situated opposite Keohane's bookshop. Another family business. Take a window seat in Conlon's, order up a mess of chowder, watch the books across the way. Last time I was in, Martin Sheen was tucking into cod and chips. Nobody paid him a blind bit of notice. Despite *The West Wing* being de rigueur viewing for most of the city and all the young girls with renewed crushes on Rob Lowe.

Me, I liked Toby, the intense Jewish worrier. Stands to reason. When God was bestowing "Lighten Up" on babies, he skipped me. Probably knew I was destined for the guards.

For the Spanish Arch, I strapped on the Walkman; Bono launched into "One". Wanted to roar along with him. If U2 have had their day, where does that leave me?

The copy of *Tales of Ordinary Madness* was published by City Lights and beautifully produced. The feel, bind, print are all part of the value. Magical photo of Bukowski on the cover, smoking a cheroot, his face looking destroyed, but in an interesting fashion. You don't think ruined; you think lived to the burn. I got an espresso takeaway and sat on the steps, a Thai restaurant to my rear. How Irish is that?

Began to read. Bono had given way to Johnny Duhan's *Flame,* his most intense, personal album. Not easy listening.

I glanced back at Quay Street. Teeming with tourists and not noon yet. How the city had changed. When I was a child, this was one of the most depressed and depressive areas. Renowned for two things: a pawnshop and the Kasbah.

A man went drinking on Saturday, in his best suit; Monday, the suit went into the pawn. Depending on the rent man, it stayed a few days or a month.

The Kasbah had its own glory. Beyond a dive, it was run by Nora Crubs, and you did not fuck with her.

Ever.

When the pubs closed, you knocked at the Kasbah. Admittance depended purely on whim. Once inside, you could have a drink, the whole point of the exercise. What you also got was a plate of pigs' trotters, the aforementioned "Crubeens". The taste was primarily of salt. There's a lot to be said for salt.

It was a favourite spot of the guards, big country lads who always called for seconds. In these days of multicultural population, I don't think the non-Europeans would have appreciated the menu.

A shadow fell. I looked up to see a ban garda. She said,

"You'll have to move along, sir."

Before I could protest, she broke into a smile. I recognised the girl from our encounter in McSwiggan's. Reached for the name, said,

"Ridge . . . right?"

Sigh, then,

"I told you, it's Nic an Iomaire. We don't do English."

"Like I give a fuck."

The expletive rocked her. She rallied, said,

"I could do you for offensive language."

"Go for it."

She looked round, then,

"I need to talk to you."

"No."

"Excuse me?"

"I don't want to talk to you, Ridge."

"It's important . . . I'll buy you drink."

"Where?"

"Anywhere you like."

"Brennan's Yard?"

Hesitation, then,

"Isn't that dear?"

"You mean expensive? Yeah . . . so I hear."

"All right . . . tomorrow night . . . half eight?"

"I'll be there."

"I better go. I don't want to be seen talking to you."

She turned to go, and I said,

"Ridge!"

"Yes?"

"Don't wear the uniform."

I was watching the England–Greece World Cup qualifier. Beckham as captain had just scored the most amazing goal. With Schole's previous one, it was a Greek goodbye. The English commentator had gone ballistic. Even the Mohawk hairstyle of Beckham was nearly forgiven. The phone rang. I said,

"Yeah."

One eye on the television.

"Hey, big boy."

"Hello, Kirsten."

"What are you doing?"

"Watching football."

"Want to play with me?"

I sighed. Not in my mother's class but heartfelt, said,

"Not really."

"Aw, come on, Jack, you're no fun."

"I am invited to a party though."

"Oh, I do love to party."

"Meet you here in an hour."

"I'm counting the minutes."

Click.

Turned the telly off. Had a tepid shower, did some 'ludes and surveyed my vast wardrobe. Figured white shirt, jeans and sweater; maybe wear the sweater over my shoulder, hanging loose. If I'd shades, I could perch them on my head and be the total asshole. No, the forecast was rain . . . a real surprise . . . so dug out my garda all-weather coat. Unlike me, it improved with age. Turned the collar up . . . get that edge. Checked the mirror and realized, I'd become my father.

When did that happen?

I took out the Heckler & Koch and smelled the barrel. You'd know it had been fired recently. I wrapped it in oilcloth, got on my knees and stashed it between the springs of the mattress. If Janet got round to that level of cleaning, she'd get the land of her life.

Back to the wardrobe, I took out the GHB, the liquid E I'd got from Stewart, the drug dealer. He'd been adamant about the correct dosage. If your evening includes a possible husband killer and a gay party, then you need all the help available. I put it in my pocket.

Took the stairs and hung around the lobby.

A yellow Datsun pulled up, the door opened, and I saw a long nyloned leg. If Kirsten had a shorter skirt, she'd have been arrested. It was made of shiny PVC, and she'd a sleeveless halter top. In red. Her hair was tousled. I'm fond of that word. Suggests bed and heavy to heavier sex. Mrs Bailey was at reception. She said,

"The word hussy springs to mind."

That is not a word I'm fond of. I stepped outside, and Kirsten did a pirouette, asked,

"Like it?"

"It's hard to miss."

Two young lads passing went,

"Jesus."

She gave them a huge smile. I said,

"I'm not travelling in a yellow car."

"Is it too much?"

"Doesn't accessorise."

"It's a rental. We'll walk."

She linked my arm, and her perfume did giddy things to my head. She said,

"Paris."

"What?"

"My scent."

"You're a mind-reader now?"

"Only the dirty ones."

As we drew near Terence's place, she stopped, said,

"Hold on a goddamn minute."

"Yeah?"

"Terence lives this way."

"It's his party, he'll cry if he wants to."

She glared, said,

"You're bringing me to a party given by that Nancy boy?"

"He said it was a seventies theme. You seem a seventies kind of girl. Was I wrong?"

She examined me closely, asked,

"What are you on?"

"Excuse me?"

"Come on, Taylor, I know the score. It's not coke; you don't have the motor mouth. Something softer . . . double valium?"

"Quaaludes."

She was delighted, near screamed,

"They're still making them! Shit, where's my Eagles albums?"

We had reached Terry's place on Merchant's Road, another dead-end street of my youth, now a line of flash apartments and businesses like cosmetic surgery. His building was constructed from that fine Connemara granite. Hewn out of the stubborn

ground to become a façade for the new rich. I rang the bell and
we were buzzed through. Kirsten said,

"I can't believe I'm going to this little prick's party."

"I didn't think women used that word."

"How else do you think we stay amused?"

The party had spilled out into the corridor, and yes, that seventies theme was evident. Flares, nay elephant flares, stacked
heels, crushed velvet jackets and big hair. On both sexes. The
music sounded suspiciously like "Ballroom Blitz".

I wish I didn't know that.

Pushed our way through as Kirsten said,

"Your era evidently."

Someone handed me a joint and I took a hit, offered it to
Kirsten, who said,

"I don't do strange spittle, at least not with an audience."

Terence appeared. Tight yellow shirt and skintight yellow
flares with a wide red belt. I said,

"He matches your car."

Sweat was pouring from his headband. Big smile till he saw
my "date", then,

"Are you out of your fucking mind?"

I offered the spliff, said,

"Chill, man."

A Spaniard in his twenties, impossibly good looking, came
up, took Terence's hand, said,

"I am Geraldo."

"Like Gerald?"

"Sí."

I think he'd served me coffee on Quay Street. He was wearing a black silk shirt and pants to match and a huge gold chain
round his neck. Now that you could have taken to the pawn,
got them excited.

Gerald extended his arms, said,

"The wet bar is in the corner."

Terence stomped off, saying,

"I'll see you later, Taylor."

I turned to Kirsten, said,

"He didn't call you Mum."

The barman I recognised from O'Neachtain's. He leaned over, whispered,

"I'm not gay."

"Did I say a word?"

"No . . . but . . ."

He indicated the same sex couples, already partying down, said,

"I wouldn't want you to think . . ."

"I think we'd like a drink."

"Gotcha . . . for the lady?"

"Scotch rocks. Make it two."

He did.

The music was now Gary Glitter: "Do You Want to Be in My Gang?"

Kirsten said,

"They play Village People and I'm, like, outa here."

I laughed, and she said,

"A man sets out to draw the world. As the years go by, he peoples a space with images of provinces, kingdoms, mountains, bays, ships, islands, fish, rooms, instruments, stars, horses and individuals. A short time before he dies, he discovers that the patient labyrinth of lines traces the lineaments of his own face."

She stopped, knocked back the scotch like a docker. Having seen a lot of the docks recently, I knew. I said,

"Impressive."

"It's by Jorge Luis Borges . . . *El Hacedor*."

"You should run it by Geraldo."

"Please, he couldn't spell dick, no pun intended."

I thought of Jeff and his Dylan piece and wondered why people were memorising such odd stuff, asked,

"And what, you learnt that piece by heart? Why?"

"No choice."

"They're teaching Borges now?"

Gave me a cool, slow, languid look. The scotch had already hit her, giving her sensuality, always simmering, a blatant edge. She said,

"Whoa, down boy. You're always reaching conclusions. Nothing is ever as it appears. My husband, my dear departed, had it pinned above the bathroom mirror. I guess it stuck."

"YMCA" began, to delighted shrieks from the crowd. Kirsten pushed the empty glass into my hand, said,

"I warned you."

And was gone.

Went after her. My arm grabbed in the corridor. Terry, now seriously dehydrated, shouted,

"What's your game, Taylor?"

"A ploy . . . face to face with her accuser, she might confess."

"You're full of shit."

"That, too."

"And you remain, inviolate."

Johnny Duhan, "Inviolate"

Kirsten was heading fast towards the Augustinian. A very drunk businessman was swaying at the door of his BMW, singing "A Galway Girl".

Last time I'd heard it, Steve Earle had been on stage in the Town Hall. This guy was beeping the locks of the car in time to the song, on, beep, off, beep, hiccup,

Like that.

He appeared deliriously happy.

Envy writ large, I swallowed, shouted,

"Kirsten . . . Jeez."

Caught her at the top of Buttermilk Lane. She said,

"Terry shouted 'whore' at me before I left, then he spat."

"Christ."

"I told him to relax, unless he wanted a heart attack."

She hailed a taxi, asked,

"You coming?"

"Sure."

The cab driver told us why the people rejected the Nice Treaty, said,

"Can't have Europe bullying us, am I right?"

No one answered him. Kirsten gave him directions, and undeterred he went on to discuss the Danes. At the house, she hopped out, said,

"Pay him."

And disappeared inside

As I rummaged for money, the driver surveyed the house, said,

"You're in there, pal."

"I'm the hired help."

He winked, then,

"Them *FÁS* courses are mighty."

And burnt rubber down the drive. I went inside; no sign of her. A shout from upstairs,

"I'm in the shower, make yourself at home."

I tried.

Found the bar, poured a scotch, plonked myself on the sofa.

A scatter of books on the table, including Jackie Collins, Alice Taylor, Maeve Binchy.

And lo and behold, a beautiful slim volume titled *The Legend of the Holy Drinker* by Joseph Roth. Translated by Michael Hofmann.

I was definitely caught.

I read the flap:

Published in 1939, the year the author died. Like Andreas, the hero of the story, Roth drank himself to death in Paris, but this is not an autobiographical confession.

I said aloud,

"Thank Christ."

And lit up a cig. No sign of an ashtray. Read on:

*It is a secular miracle tale, in which the vagrant Andreas, after liv-
ing under bridges, has a series of lucky breaks that lift him briefly
on to a different plane of existence. The novella is extraordinarily
compressed, dry-eyed and witty, despite its melancholic subject
matter.*

Published by Granta. Am I old or what? I remember when
Bill Buford began the magazine and the book he wrote, *Among
the Thugs.*

Should be mandatory for guards dealing with football hooli-
gans.

It crossed my mind to nick it. Just slip it into item 8234's vo-
luminous pocket, say nowt. I put it back on the table.

Kirsten walked in, towelling her hair. Barefoot, wearing a
short silk kimono. That's an image that's always worked for me.
It's so casually intimate. I've only glimpsed it rarely, and that is
the indictment of my isolation. I savoured it then. She glanced at
the book, said,

"Cross your mind to steal it?"

"What?"

"I know you, Jack. That's how I got it."

She moved to the bar, began fixing a drink, humming softly.
Jesus, I hate that; it's a notch below musak. Still, I thought I
recognised it, asked,

"What's that?"

"I don't know. I keep hearing it on a golden oldies station."

Came to me. I said,

"Jeez, Kevin Johnson."

"Who?"

"'Rock and Roll I Gave You All the Best Years of My
Life.'"

A bottle of Stoli held midair, she asked,

"That's a confession?"

"The name of the song."

"I like it."

"There's a line in there, sums up my years in the guards."

"What's this, Taylor, you're getting all choked up on the past?"

I ignored that, said,

"I don't remember the line exactly, but like this: 'Trying to go it solo in someone else's band'."

She poured the drink, took a hefty belt, said,

"That's you . . . the maverick."

I rooted in my pocket, asked,

"Want to do GHB?"

"Oh, punishment, you pervert."

Produced the liquid E, began,

"You have to be very careful with this."

Her eyes alight, she went,

"Fuck that, let's get it on."

We did.

All the promised effects: inhibitions, clothes and self-control did disappear.

Stewart had guaranteed it gave euphoria and libido.

He wasn't kidding.

Course he'd advised extreme caution with alcohol, but I figured care was an area I'd never given much time to. Too old to begin then.

"Fifty is a dangerous age—for all men. The man of fifty has most to say but no one will listen. His fears sound incredible because they sound so new—he might be making them up. His body alarms him; it starts playing tricks on him, his teeth warn him, his stomach scolds, he's balding at last; a pimple might be cancer; indigestion a heart attack. He's feeling an unapparent fatigue; he wants to be young but he knows he ought to be old. He's neither one and he is terrified."

Paul Theroux, *Saint Jack*

Came to in broad daylight, sat up. Where was I? In a huge bed, white silk sheets. Two things hit me: I was naked and un-hungover. No sign of Kirsten. A clock on the bedside table read 12.05.

Past noon, high or otherwise.

How long had I been out? No idea. I could recall magnificent gymnastic sex. Me! Boy, would my body pay when reality returned. But the lengthy sleep . . . An alcoholic skirts as close to insomnia as it gets. Enough booze to put down Young Munster, yet wakes after an hour, replete with hangover. The rest of the night consists of a befuddled series of fevered naps, nightmares, dread and sweats.

And waiting at daybreak, the whole sorry circus over again, *Groundhog Day* with the emphasis on hog. I didn't leap out of bed but was nearly agile. No sign of my clothes. Went to a large wardrobe, opened it.

Jesus.

One of those walk-in jobs. Must have been fifty suits, as many sports jackets and, lined in military precision, shoes. Close to a hundred. Imelda Marcos would have sung. I pulled a heavy cotton shirt and a pair of Farah slacks. Fit pretty good. Went back to the bedroom, saw my cigs, lighter on the bureau. Fired up.

The door opened and Kirsten entered with a tray. Wearing the kimono, she'd a shit-eating grin, said,

"Well good morning, stud."

I groaned.

She set the tray down. I saw toast, eggs, OJ, folded napkins and, God, a red rose. Silver coffee pot, steaming. I said,

"I'd kill for a coffee."

Malicious smile, then,

"Is that appropriate to say to a murder suspect?"

She poured and passed me the cup. It smelled fantastic. Actually tasted near as good. It's one of life's jokes that coffee never fulfils its promise. If you based your life on that truth, you'd probably become a TD. She buttered some toast, laid a wedge of egg on it, said,

"Open wide, Romeo."

Shook my head,

"I don't think so."

"You don't want me to feed you?"

"No."

"I used to feed my husband."

"And he's . . ."

She shrugged. I drank the coffee, asked,

"Where's my clothes?"

"I burned them."

"Seriously, where are they?"

"I seriously burned them."

"Christ, why?"

She turned to look at me, said,

"You're going to be with me, you're going to have to smarten up."

"I don't think so."

"You don't think you're going to smarten up . . . or you don't think you're going to be with me?"

"Both."

She pointed to the wardrobe, said,

"My husband's clothes will fit, and believe me, they're the very best. I bought them."

A thought struck me, and I grabbed her arm, shouted,

"The coat . . . my garda coat . . . did you burn that?"

"I tried . . . you're hurting me."

I tore down the stairs, the hall, through the kitchen and could see the fire in the garden. Flung the door open and approached the flames. The coat was thrown to the side, badly singed but intact. I grabbed it, the smell of smoke in my nostrils. Kirsten was at the door, hands on her hips, asking,

"What's the deal? It's a piece of shit."

"That, lady, is my history, my career, the only link to my past."

"What a pathetic history then."

I brushed past her, went through to the front room, searching. She followed and I asked,

"Where is it?"

"Where's what?"

"The GHB."

Half smile curling, she said,

"We used it all."

"Like I'll take your word for it. Where's the empty bottle?"

She waved towards the garden.

"With your clothes. Want to check?"

I took a deep breath, said,

"Kirsten, I hope that's the truth. You don't want to fuck with that stuff. It can cause a coma."

Now she was smiling, said,

"It sure set your motor running."

I went upstairs, selected a heavy pair of brogues. Tight on the toes, but hey, pain was familiar. She shadowed me all the way, asked,

"When are we getting together?"

"Kirsten . . . what do you do?"

"Do?"

"You know, with your life, during any given day."

"Shop and fuck."

"What?"

"The town is full of young guys. They give it up for the price of a drink."

I shook my head, unable to ask about condoms, protection. I truly was afraid of the answer. Instead I asked,

"So what do you want me for?"

"You amuse me."

I headed down the stairs, and she asked,

"You're going?"

"Yes."

"You think you can fuck and fly?"

Is there an answer?

I got the front door open, and she called,

"Yo, Jack."

"What?"

"That liquid E?"

"Yeah?"

"It's a killer."

The bad drop.

I'm not talking about a pint of Guinness gone sour. It's a concept I tried once to explain to Clancy, back when we were friends. It's a slice of ice in your heart. And not a bad thing, the ability to lash out at the final moment, a shard of preservation that comes into play when you're backed up, right against the wall. You don't even know you have it till it's absolutely vital.

Then, suddenly, a voice takes over, goes,

"Fuck with me . . . you have no idea of the ferocity I am capable of."

Clancy had shook his head, gone,

"Ary, that's mad talk."

He went on to become the embodiment of a very bad drop. Now, as I headed down Taylor's Hill, the voice kicked,

"So Kirsten, screw you."

And felt it.

I walked past Nile Lodge, turned at Scoil Ursa, and the Gaelic connection reminded me I had a date with a ban garda. I was looking forward to it; at least I could pretend so. A guy near the site of the Sancta Maria Hotel was playing a tin whistle, a cap for donations at his feet. If there's a worse spot to busk in Galway, I couldn't think of it. Nobody walks along that road. It's true ghostville. People shunned the area if they could. The hotel had burned to the ground with a tragic loss of life.

I found some coins in my burned coat and put them in the cap. His eyes widened and he asked,

"Are you on fire?"

"Not any more."

He ran a withered hand over his brow, said,

"I thought I was losing it."

He raised his thumb behind him, continued,

"That, you know, maybe . . . you'd come out of there."

Drink had mottled his face to a full purple, and his body gave odd tremors. I said,

"This isn't the best spot for your art."

He gave a knowing smile, said,

"Look at the moon, stop listening to the dogs in the street."

Go figure.

The circle of addiction, how it comes in many guises. I was tripping on the beat of no hangover, then looked into the face of raw alcoholism.

The mix rolls, and you never can predict what the result will be. Now it rolled the dice and churned out a coke craving.

I could see a neatly rolled line of pure white. A guy said to me once,

"Come on, Jack, it's so eighties."

Like I care about the era or am aware of current trends.

I'm mostly locked in some seventies mode when hope had an actual face.

Two lines of coke and the world throws its doors open. The white lightning across my brain, the ice drip along the back of my throat. Oh fuck, I felt my knees sag.

When the Charlie lights, you get this huge sense of purpose. Plus a bliss that convinces you of total insanity. Like that you can sing. And sing you do. It doesn't get much crazier than that.

But the downside: few crash like cokeheads do. From soaring to a descent to hell itself, thrashing, sick, paranoid. The physical side is no advertisement either: the lost eyes, the constant sniffles and the erosion of the membranes of the nose. Eventually the septum is totally eaten away.

The tabloids trot out poor Daniella Westbrook, the soap star, with malignant glee. Photos of how she used to be and then, close up, the ravaged nose. If not a deterrent, it is certainly a shot across the bow of glamour.

I'd reached the cathedral and felt the need of a quiet moment. Pushed open the thick brass door, and it clanged shut behind me. The relic of St Therese had attracted U2-type crowds, but it was silent now. I moved along a side aisle, the Stations of the Cross marking time with my feet. Knelt in a pew near the main altar.

Without thinking, I began,

"Glór don Athair . . ."

I'd learnt my prayers in Irish, and they only held true resonance if said thus. Course no more than any other frightened Catholic, I'm partial to a blast of Latin. The easy majesty talks to my peasant soul. The cathedral is built on the site of the old Galway Jail. Not only male prisoners but women, too. Outlandish sentences for petty crimes, an early echo of the malignancy of the Magdalen. A priest crossed my vision, paused, said,

"Mind if I sit?"

I wanted to say,

"Your gig."

Nodded. He sat in the seat in front. He was in his early forties, tall, with the dark features of a Spanish-Irish heritage. I stayed on my knees, nearly began,

"It's been thirty years since my last confession."

But he wasn't giving off the priest vibe. If anything, he'd an aura of quite serenity. He said,

"It's good to take a moment."

"It is."

"Are you a guard . . . a somewhat burned guard?"

He smiled, and I went,

"Burnt out."

"I've been there."

And he put out his hand, said,

"Tom."

"Jack Taylor."

I didn't feel the urge, the in-bred traditional knee-jerk "Father". In fact, I felt he wouldn't go for it. He said,

"Sometimes it's as much as I can do to get out of bed."

My turn to smile, say,

"Kind of your job though."

He raised his eyes to heaven. It seems to hold an added dimension when a cleric does it. He said,

"Sermons, they're the bane of my life. Telling ordinary decent people how to live when their lives are riddled with harsh reality."

"You could tell the truth."

He wasn't shocked, even taken aback, said,

"I did, once."

"And?"

"The bishop sent for me."

"Oh, oh."

"Asked me if I was practising disobedience."

I thought about that, said,

"Sounds like the guards."

He grinned, went,

"Something tells me you didn't toe the line."

"Not exactly. I smacked a guy in the mouth."

He savoured that. I asked,

"Where is the Church on suicide these days?"

He gave me the concerned look. I held up my hands, said,

"Not me . . . a friend of mine hanged himself."

He made the sign of the cross. I wasn't sure if I should do the same. He said,

"You're asking the wrong question."

"Am I?"

"Shouldn't you wonder where God stands on the subject?"

"Where does He stand?"

"I think God has tremendous compassion for a person in such a terrible frame of mind."

"Hope you're right."

He stood up, held out his hand, said,

"I enjoyed meeting you, Jack."

I took his hand, answered,

"You did me good . . . Father."

Big smile, then,

"It's supposed to be my job."

"Well, it's a long time since a priest did me any good."

He turned, genuflected in front of the altar and was gone. I headed out. At the main door, a nun was tidying pamphlets. She glared at me. I said,

"Excuse me?"

"What?"

"Fr Tom, what's his surname?"

"There's no Fr Tom."

I described him, and she said,

"Are you deaf? There's no such priest in this parish."

"Why wouldn't I have paranoid traits, living as I has lived? As my life went on, my mini paranoia would save my life more than once."

Edward Bunker, *Memoirs of a Renegade*

I didn't get back to Bailey's till late afternoon. You take a walk through Shop Street, you better not be in a hurry. You meet your past, remnants of a shaky present and forebodings of the dark future. The past is represented by school friends, who appear old, shook and furtive. The present dances in a swirl of rain, refugees and lost winos, the future through the number of mobile phones and the hieroglyphics of text. An overall effect of bewilderment.

Years ago, a radio programme called *Dear Frankie* ruled the waves. Frankie sounded like Bette Davis on a particularly bad day. The whole country knew the show. Problems sent to her seemed more ordinary, more solvable. Her answers were terse, acidic and shut down the prospect of long debate. Interspersed with commercials were snatches of Sinatra. You couldn't call her anything as lofty as the nation's conscience, but she did seem to embody a combination of good humour with scathing wit. Behind the gruffness, you got the impression she cared.

It seemed a long time since you could say anyone gave a toss.

During the terrible events of my previous case, a bright light had briefly shone. I'd met a young girl named Laura, a very young girl. In her twenties, when you're hitting fifty, that's near as young as it gets.

Worse, she was very keen.

I can't say I was totally smitten, but I sure liked her a lot. She did the almost impossible, made me feel good about myself. What drugs and alcohol provided was an ease from the demons. She supplied a whole natural feeling. Who knows what it might have become. I was on the precipice of the most tragic judgement of my life. Too, I was barely over the speedy termination of my marriage. These are hardly sufficient explanation, but it's where I was.

Her mother confronted me publicly, saying,

"You should be ashamed of yourself. Laura is young enough to be your daughter."

Did I stand up to her, fight my corner and declare I was prepared to do anything to keep Laura?

Did I fuck?

I slunk away like a scalded child. Worse, rang Laura and told her I'd met someone else.

Brave . . . huh?

I had seen her a few times since, only in the distance. Once near Supermac's, she'd stopped, but I turned on my heel, moved fast away. Time heals most things or reaches an accommodation whereby you can function. Jeez, how I long for the truth of that. No amount of years will clear away the shabbiness of my behaviour.

I've tried to lump it among the other debris of a road badly travelled. Doesn't cut it. Dislodges itself from the warehouse of shame, to stand alone and cry,

"You acted appallingly."

The moving finger, having writ, has not moved on.

Kafka, in his diaries, said,

The man who is lost in his own lifetime is able to see more things and to see them in greater detail. With one hand, he tries to ward off despair, with the other, he records all that he is able to see.

From all of this, I learnt one simple thing.

Times are, I'm a bad bastard.

When I got back to Bailey's, I was close to beat. Mrs Bailey was behind her desk, said,

"I saw Dana today."

Surely there's a coherent reply. I waved vaguely and took the stairs. Thought,

"Gonna grab me some shut-eye."

Opened my door to a scene of chaos. The room was destroyed. My books, torn, were scattered on the floor, the bed upturned and deep gashes in the mattress. Clothes were strewn everywhere and ripped asunder. A strong smell of urine came from the ruined wardrobe. The curtains had been jammed in the sink.

I closed the door, tried to get my mind in gear. Moved through the wreckage and checked the springs of the bed. The gun was gone.

In the wardrobe, I'd previously gone to great pains to lift a board and stash the drugs. Lifted it and let out a small sigh of relief. They hadn't been touched.

Grabbed two heavy-duty tabs and dry swallowed them.

Moved to the sink in search of a water glass. It was in smithereens. I pulled the sodden curtain away and let it slump to the floor. Bent my head and drank from the tap. Straightening, I reached for my cigs, fired one up. Gazed at the heap of clothes. Jeez, did I have the energy to shop anew? I kept having to start over. The prized collection of books made me want to weep. Not only were they torn but appeared to have been savagely mutilated, pieces of covers barely visible. The backbone of whatever education I had . . . Merton, Chandler, Yeats.

Poets, crime writers, philosophers, chancers, all woven together in a mess of destruction. I'd rarely find a better epitaph for my life.

Kiki, my ex-wife, had tried to give me a crash course in philosophy, to get me to think.

I'd protested,

"What I most want is not to think. What do you suppose the oceans of booze are for?"

She'd persisted.

Course, I seized on any shard of despair, any piece of damage. I couldn't pronounce Kierkegaard with any degree of confidence, but I did remember this:

The greater the despair in one's life, the more one is able to see.

By my reckoning, my vision now should be all encompassing. Alas, nothing could be further from the truth. Was I clogged with self-pity? You betcha.

Alongside whining, dreaming and shite talk, it's what an alcoholic does best.

I trudged downstairs, approached Mrs Bailey. She gave a tentative smile and my heart sank. I said,

"I've some disturbing news."

"Ah, don't tell me you're off to London again."

"No . . . no. My room has been trashed."

"Trashed?"

"Ransacked . . . broken into. It's been gutted."

"The pups."

"What?"

"Ah, the blackguards who are loose today. No respect for anything."

"I'll pay for the damage."

"Go way our that. Let the insurance cover it."

"You're insured?"

"No, but I always wanted to say that."

THE MAGDALEN

The other sound you heard in the laundry was coughing. Like a chorus from hell. The girls all chain-smoked; it relieved the tedium and gave them a sense of being adult. The fumes in the place, combined with the nicotine, produced the racking cough from the very depths of despair. When Lucifer heard that sound, she began to smile, without even realising it. The smile began at the corner of her eyes and spread in step as she stalked the length of the room. The girls, heads down, tried to gauge her mood. Course it was always foul, but the level of her wrath varied.

Her favourite trick was to select a girl and ask her to sew a pile of curtains. She'd almost sweet-talk the creature, then from nowhere, she'd lash out with a fist and send the girl spinning, as she screamed,

"You whore of Babylon, where do you think you are? This isn't a spa. You're here to repent, and if I ever catch you smiling again, it's the toilet for you."

Among her catalogue of cruelty was the wrapping of wet sheets around the offender and leaving her to stand all night thus. She called it the "cleansing".

I went to the AIB and joined the queue. Took the time to fill out a withdrawal slip. Put down a hefty figure. Wouldn't you know, the same cashier. I said brightly,

"Hi."

She looked up and remembered. She didn't sigh, 'cause the banker's manual forbids that. But she got as close as she could. I handed her the docket, said,

"I guess you won't require proof of identity this time."

She could delay me though. That is in the manual. She stood, said,

"I'll need this authorised."

"Grab a cig while you can."

"I don't smoke."

"You amaze me."

I read about home loans, equities and other riveting shit. Could see her in consultation with a suit. He looked my way four times. I know because I counted. When she returned, she asked,

"How would you like your cash?"

"In a brown envelope, keep things familiar."

Gave me a white one, and I said,

"You've a touch of the bad drop."

Went to Dunne's, Oxfam, Age Concern and Penney's. Bought

> 2 suits
>
> 3 jeans
>
> 6 shirts
>
> 4 Ts
>
> 3 shoes.

And blitzkrieged through what had been a fat lump of money. Hailed a cab, and the driver said,

"Yo . . . Jack."

"How ya doing?"

"Not as good as you. What's with all the parcels?"

"New start. Listen, could you leave all of this at Bailey's Hotel?"

"You bought new gear for the staff?"

I pulled off a wedge, said,

"And a drink for yourself."

No more questions.

Next to the Augustinian and lit a rake of candles for Brendan Flood. Is there a difference between one and eight being lit? Yeah . . . eases that nagging conscience. I didn't know what prayer to offer, so I said,

"I miss you, Brendan."

If not the most profound, it was certainly the most truthful.

Then to Charlie Byrne's. Clothes might be essential but books were vital. And it's my favourite place. Charlie on his way out, said,

"Jack, there's a whole new load of crime fiction just arrived."

"Brilliant."

"I put your favourites aside."

Now some people know bookies and believe it makes a difference. I don't really think they'll put a good horse aside for you, and yes, they surely do know about favourites.

Give me a bookseller every time. Inside, Vinny was reading *Meetings with Remarkable Men*.

I asked,

"Is that for show or are you . . . like seriously into it?"

He gave a huge smile.

"It's for serious show. Where have you been? We thought you'd given up books."

I stretched out my hands, palms up, asked,

"How can you give up books?"

"That's what we like to hear."

"Vinny, I've lost my current library."

"Lost?"

"It's a long story."

"Got you. So . . . you'll want to start over, get the basics in."

"Will I run through a list?"

"No, I'll get you up and flying. Where are you based?"

If he was surprised, he didn't show it. I said,

"Can you deliver in a few days?"

He was writing in a pad, said,

"I'll even bring a pizza."

I reached for my wallet, and he said,

"Let's do that after."

That evening, I was back in my partially restored room. It still looked rough, but the devastation had been curtailed. I asked Mrs Bailey,

"Who did the repairs?"

"Janet and I."

"What?"

"Sure, you couldn't get tradesmen for a week. I could move you to another room."

"No . . . no . . . that's great."

My clothes had been delivered. I showered and tried on a new suit. In the cracked mirror, my reflection was jagged. The sections of the suit I could see seemed OK. My face appeared fragmented, and I definitely blamed the glass. Time to go and meet the ban garda. As I got downstairs, Mrs Bailey asked,

"Did you tell the guards?"

"No."

"I didn't think you would."

In 1982, Pope John Paul II, addressing a group of garda pilgrims, said,

> In the contemporary world the task of the police is certainly not an easy one. It requires a sense of vocation, of committed dedication to the safety and well being of your fellow citizens. It requires that you recognize and consider yourselves as an important and effective moral force for good at work in your society.

I could recite the above by heart and did so at the oddest times.

When Brennan's Yard was opened, the general response was,

"You're kidding."

Who'd call a hotel after a yard? But it's been doing good. Round the corner from Quay Street, it does a brisk trade. Sure, it has notions, but they're not flash notions. The bar doesn't require a suit, but it whispers the suggestion.

I went in, and an eager barman hailed,

"Good evening, sir."

Like I said . . . notions.

I got a pint of Guinness and took a table at the rear. Didn't recognize the ban garda when she appeared dressed in denim top, short black skirt and medium heels, a drink in her hand. I said,

"I wouldn't know you in that gear."

"Can I sit?"

"Unless you're happier standing."

She sat.

I looked at her drink, said,

"Let me guess, a spritzer?"

"No, white wine."

I lit a cig and she said,

"Could you please not smoke?"

"Jeez, Ridge, what kind of tight ass are you?"

"The kind who doesn't enjoy passive smoking."

I leant back, had a hard look. She had nice features in a bland fashion. You wouldn't pick her out of a crowd, but I felt she wanted it that way. I said,

"You asked to see me. I don't remember you saying there'd be rules."

She took a sip of the wine. Impossible to say if she derived any satisfaction. Her eyes had the fevered shine of the dedicated. Not a zealot but in the neighbourhood. Her voice was quiet as she said,

"Why do you like annoying people?"

"I don't . . . not really. Let's say I don't like 'annoying people'. And God knows, they're thick on the ground. Prosperity's made them worse."

"You prefer the good old days."

"Don't be snide, Ridge, it twists your mouth."

She watched as I finished the pint, said,

"Could you stay sober till we have our talk?"

"Depends how long winded you are."

She leaned forward, said,

"I'm good at what I do."

"So was I."

She shook her head, went,

"I'm serious. I love being a guard. I don't sneer at the force."

Pause,

"Like you do."

I stood, asked,

"You want a drink?"

"No."

As I ordered, I tried to rein in my temper. No question, she got to me. I lit another cig, checked to see if she was watching.

No.

Staring out the window. Probably dreaming of one day being the chief. It crossed my mind to hammer the drink, then fuck off. Leave her to the high moral ground. Knew she wasn't the type to let it be. Some other day she'd waylay me, and I'd have to hear whatever it was she wanted to say. A priest came bustling in, Fr Malachy, my mother's friend. He spotted me, said,

"Propping up the bar as usual."

"And you're being an asshole as usual."

He stepped back, my bitterness assaulting him, but he rallied, said,

"I thought here would be a cut above your station."

"They let you in."

"It's the sodality dinner. We have a room booked."

"Prayer pays, eh?"

"Your mother is poorly. You might sober up enough to visit."

I grabbed my pint, began to move, said,

"For that visit, I'd need to be very drunk."

When I sat down, Ridge said,

"Is that a priest?"

"No, that's the dregs of the barrel. So, what's on your mind?"

"The Magdalen."

"And . . ."

"Galway is a European city now."

"So?"

"So, there are people who'd prefer not to have old history on display again."

"What's this to do with me?"

"You were searching for a woman who worked there."

"And you know this how?"

"My uncle . . . was a guard."

"Jeez, a family of ye."

"I can help you."

"You're a little late. I already found her."

"You're not listening."

"To what? The case is closed; it's a done deal."

She took a deep breath, said,

"Two young men have been murdered in the city recently."

"Yeah, I heard it on the news."

"And that's all you know?"

I was getting exasperated, near shouted,

"What the hell else is there to know?"

"Their names?"

"Why should I want to know that?"

She sat back, waited, then,

"Because they're related to Rita Monroe . . . her nephews."

I tried to get my head round this information, muttered,

"Are you sure?"

"What do you think?"

"Jesus."

I went back through what I knew, or thought I knew, asked,

"Why would anyone want to kill her nephews?"

"To hurt her."

Then I recalled the time I'd met Rita Monroe. She'd said,

"I'm not feeling well. There's been a bereavement."

Or words to that effect. And she'd been very shook up. I, of course, had completely ignored that. Too, her house had been ransacked, as had my room. Ridge said,

"You look like you've seen a ghost."

"Let me think."

The name that came to mind, the common denominator, was Bill Cassell. But he wanted to thank her, to express his gratitude for the help she had given his mother. I asked,

"What do you know about Rita Monroe?"

Ridge opened her handbag, took out a notebook, flipped through some pages, said,

"The Magdalen girls called her Lucifer, the devil incarnate. No one rained down abuse and torment like she did."

My head reeled. Bill Cassell had told me she was an angel, and I just outright accepted that. Never once had it struck me to check out his story. I was so anxious to be free of my debt, I'd have stood on my head. I asked,

"How did you find out about her?"

"My uncle suggested I do some checking."

"Oh . . . the guard."

"That's right."

"How come he's so fucking smart?"

"Was."

"What?"

"Was so . . . as you put it . . . f-in' . . . smart. He's dead."

"I'm sorry. Were you close?"

"Were you?"

"Excuse me?"

"To my Uncle Brendan . . . Flood."

"But your name . . ."

"He was my mother's brother."

I didn't know what to say, said,

"I don't know what to say."

She sipped some more wine, said,

"He thought you could have been a great guard. Even in your current occupation, you managed to impress him, despite . . ."

She didn't finish so I asked,

"What?"

"Despite your weaknesses."

"Yes, well, I've plenty."

"That's what he said."

My glass was empty. I debated another trip to the bar. She said,

"He told me to contact you if ever he was 'unavailable'. That you needed a contact, a connection to the guards. He called it your lifeline."

I had to ask, so,

"Were you surprised he . . . did what he did?"

"Killed himself?"

"Yes."

"I was shocked, but I don't know if I was totally surprised. He was a man who needed to passionately believe in something. You probably don't understand that."

I held the empty glass, asked,

"You think I have no beliefs?"

"Alcohol . . . that's all you have."

"Nice. You'll go far in the force; they appreciate thickness."

"Uncle Brendan respected you and seemed to like you."

"Which you don't."

"I hate waste."

"Jesus, you're some ball-buster."

"If you're going to fumble around in the Magdalen case, I felt you should at least know what's going on."

"Thanks."

She stood up, said,

"I didn't do it for you."

"Right."

She placed a card on the table, said,

"My phone numbers, home and mobile. If there's anything I can do for you."

"You could order me a pint as you leave."

"Order it yourself."

And she was gone.

I lit a cig and muttered,

"Oh, fuck."

I knew I had a whole mess of figuring out to do, but I couldn't get my mind in gear. Her revelations had sucker-punched me. Stood up and thought,

"I'm right beside Sweeney's now."

The docks were out the door and turn right. You could hear the seagulls with that shrill sound of annoyance. Bill's local was that near. What was I going to do . . . or say to him?

No idea.

Fr Malachy was on the path, sucking on a cig. I said,

"The sodality is a no smoking zone?"

"Some of us respect the feelings of others."

I took a long look at him till he snapped,

"What?"

"You'd have made a fine guard."

"Better than you anyway."

"No, really, you have the cut of them."

"God called first."

I began to move away, said,

"I'm not certain of much, but I'm convinced it wasn't God."

Whatever he shouted after me, I didn't hear it. Nothing up-lifting anyway. Your life is in some bizarre state when priests are throwing abuse at you on the street.

"Too harsh a push, to do this stuff alone."

K.B.

Sweeney's was closed. No sign of any activity. A guy was pass-ing, and I asked him what had happened. He said,

"Sold. Just like everything else in the town. They'll have luxury apartments up in no time. That's what we need, more frigging apartments."

The books arrived from Charlie Byrne's, an eclectic mix of poetry, crime, philosophy, biography. Vinny had managed to mostly obtain hardbacks. There's a world of difference between them and paperbacks. The only merit I've ever found in the latter is the price. Among the poets were Rilke, Coleridge, Lowell, Yeats. The crime had the foundation of Thompson, Cain, Chandler, Derek Raymond. I didn't pay much attention to the philosophers, simply stacked them against the wall. My frame of mind could hardly register titles, let alone content. Biography had a fine mix: Fitzgerald, Graham Greene, Rupert Graves, Branson.

Branson!

I slung that. I could see the smile on Vinny's face. Knew it would knock a rise out of me. A knock on the door. I said,

"Yeah?"

Janet came in, looking even more fragile than ever. She asked,

"Do you need any help in arranging your books?"

"No, I enjoy the job."

She peered at the various stacks, said,

"You're a holy terror for reading."

"Thanks, I think."

"Will you read them all?"

"I sure hope so."

"I'm reading a book."

"Are you . . . that's good . . . would I know it?"

"A life of Matt Talbot."

"Oh."

I thought,

"Jesus, him again."

A light in her eyes as she said,

"He'd been a martyr to the drink. When he stopped, he used to scourge himself."

I nearly said,

"I've been fairly scourged myself."

A hesitancy in her expression, then,

"I could lend it to you."

I indicated the books, said,

"Maybe not right now, but hey . . ."

I moved across the room, retrieved the discarded volume, said,

"This is for you."

She stared at the cover, said,

"Richard Branson."

"Another remarkable man."

She was unsure and who could blame her? She said,

"My husband might read it."

"Terrific."

"Thank you, Mr Taylor."

When she'd gone, I surveyed my library. Definitely improved the room. Most of all, what they gave me was reassurance. I put on my second new suit and felt I was halfway to being a citizen. Outside, a light drizzle was coming down. In Galway, that's almost a fine day. Decided not to go back for my all-weather coat. My plan was to find Bill Cassell and revisit Rita Monroe.

I was throwing this around in my mind as I walked up Eglington Street. Nearing the chemist, I heard shouting. A man was roaring at his children. He was over six foot, broad, and with a face suffused with rage. I don't know what the kids had done, but they were clearly now in the grip of total terror. They couldn't have been more than four or five years old. As I neared, the man leaned down and began to lash the boy across the face. The boy's sister screamed,

"Daddy . . . Daddy . . . don't."

He smacked her on the head. I said,

"Hey."

He turned, hand raised again, said,

"Fuck off."

I looked round. People were staring. The man's hand began its descent. I grabbed his arm and he turned, tried to head-butt me. That's the first thing you learn as a guard on the street. At Templemore you hear about it; on the street, you learn how to fend it.

I stepped to the side and said,

"Take it easy."

He didn't seem drunk. That would have been simple to quell. His eyes were steady but aglow with meanness. I'd seen their type and knew that reasoning was out of the question. Brutality was their currency. I moved back, and he gave a small smile, said,

"I'm going to break your fucking neck."

Rushed me. I swung low with my right, caught him solid in the stomach. Could have left it at that; he wasn't going to be roaring any more. A suspended moment, as there has been throughout my life, when I could have pulled back from the recklessness that has blasted through my existence. Think I saw the little girl's face, the fear he had put there, but it wasn't just that. He was a bully, and I was sick of them.

Took a step, then, leaning into it with my shoulder and all my weight, I launched with my left hand. The force hit him under the chin, up off his feet, sent him crashing through the plate glass window of the chemist. The people gathered gave a collective "Ah".

They say there are two types of people in jail. The first adapt well, control the cigarette trade, prey on the weak and thrive on the petty rituals. The second are totally unable to adapt. Are wounded and hunted from their first moment.

And the one sure person who should never go to jail is a policeman.

Both of the above are higher on the food chain than a disgraced cop. It's payback time for the inmates and complete contempt from the wardens.

Within minutes of my lashing out, two squad cars arrived and an ambulance. Guards grabbed me, bundled me into the back of the car. I glanced at my hand, bruising already spreading across the knuckles. We didn't leave then. No, the guards took statements. People stared in at me, a mix of excitement and cruelty on their faces. Did not bode well for what they were relating.

What I most remember of the scene, though, is the face of the little girl. Backlit by the broken window, she appeared to be forgotten in the turmoil. She stared at me with huge eyes, her thumb in her mouth. Her image is burned on my soul. If I had to describe her expression, I can only say it was pure hatred. I can't blame the father for that. I was taken to the barracks, charged and led to a cell. It had two bunks. A man, sleeping or unconscious, occupied one; I sat on mine, tried to catch my breath. The suit had a tear in the sleeve and already appeared as if someone had slept in it. A fatigue hit me, but I didn't want to sleep. Jesus, to nap and then come to in a cell . . . I stood and moved to the window. Through the bars, I could see a bare wall. I'd taken two tranquillizers that morning, their effect long dissipated.

Tremors ran up my chest, turned, ran down my arms. Tried to identify a sound I was hearing. Oh God, the grinding of my teeth. If I ever got out, I'd have a bath in liquid E. An hour passed, and I paced back and forth. The man in the other bunk ranted in his sleep, loud streams of obscenities, punctuated by sighs. Hard to say which was worse. At one stage, he began to vomit, and I turned him to prevent his suffocating. He clawed at my face. When I had him turned, I sank on the bed in near exhaustion. The smell of raw alcohol in the air was nearly overpowering. I felt it gag in my mouth. It being that rare of rarest days, not a drop had I taken. More time passed and the cell began to darken. Then the lights flicked and bathed us in harsh unyielding light. I paced anew. A guard appeared, began to unlock the gate, said,

"Come on, you're wanted."

As I moved, he warned,

"No funny business . . . hear?"

I nodded.

He led me to an interview room and left, locking the door. There was a metal table, two chairs and a seriously misshapen ashtray. When I'd been charged, the contents of my pockets had been emptied, put in an envelope. I'd have murdered for a cigarette and caused untold mayhem for a pill, not to mention a double scotch. I sat on a hard chair, tried not to consider my situation. The door opened and Clancy breezed in. A shit-eating grin plastered on his face. He seemed elated, said,

"Well, well, well."

"That's a neat line. You should jot it down, trot it out at one of those golf club functions."

His uniform was pressed to perfection. If anything, his grin widened. He said,

"Didn't I tell you, boyo, one of these days you'd fuck up big time and I'd have you."

"I don't suppose due process applies."

He cupped his hand to one ear, asked,

"What's that, boyo. Speak up . . . don't worry about shouting; there isn't a soul will disturb us."

"Don't I get a solicitor, a phone call?"

He loved that, answered in an awful parody of an American accent,

"As the Yanks say, 'Who you gonna call?' "

I waited, as if I'd any choice. He said,

"The fellah you put through the window, you couldn't have picked a worse one."

"I wasn't exactly checking references."

Big guffaw. He truly did seem to be having himself a time, said,

"You're priceless, Jack. But yer man, the window fellah, guess who he is."

"I've no idea."

"Ah, go on, guess."

"I could care less."

His hand slammed down on the table.

"Begin to care. He's one of the top businessmen in the town. He was one of the 'Man of the Year' nominations."

My turn for a half smile, answered,

"I can see where he might have been."

Now he sat. The table between us, his eyes bored into mine. He said,

"You won't like prison, Jack."

"I'd say you're right."

"More to the point, prison won't like you. Especially when they hear you were a guard."

"No doubt you'll spread the word."

"Story like that, Jack, gets round like wildfire."

I didn't answer. When they come to gloat, it's as well to let them rip, get it done. He added,

"They'll be lining up for you, Jack, know what I mean?"

He stood, asked,

"You've enough tea, cigarettes . . . have you?"

He let his eyes sweep the empty table, said,

"And no doubt you've already made a connection for your drug habit. They say you can score almost anything in prison. I have to go, a round of golf before dinner."

He banged on the door, looked back at me, said,

"I'd like to throw you some lifeline, some words of comfort in your darkest hour."

I met his eyes, said,

"On account of how we were friends once?"

"Alas, all I can offer is . . . if you think it's bad now, it's going to get much worse."

The door opened and he was gone. I was taken back to my cell. The guy in the other bunk was snoring peacefully. Maybe the worst was over for him. A few hours later, a sergeant appeared in the corridor. He was in his fifties, his bad fifties. Moving over to the cell, he said,

"Jack . . . here . . . sorry I didn't get down sooner."

Passed me a Dunne's bag, added,

"I didn't want the young crowd to see these."

And he was gone.

I couldn't recall his name. The face had a vague familiarity, but I couldn't say from when. Opened the bag: cigs and lighter, sandwiches, bottle of Paddy.

Wilfred Scawen Blunt was a prisoner in Galway Jail in 1888. He noted that in the jail:

There had been a pleasant feeling . . . between the prisoners and warders, due to the fact that they . . . were much of the same class, peasants born with the same natural ideas, virtues, vices and weaknesses.

From *The Women of Galway Jail* by Geraldine Curtin.

I rationed the whiskey, taking small sips, enough to ease me down. Held off on a cigarette till the artificial calm had begun. Then lit one. Ah . . . the hit . . . Was even able to contemplate the sandwiches. Not actually eat but at least consider the proposition. Stowed everything under the pillow.

When a young guard came to check, he eyed me suspiciously. If he'd come in to search, I'd have fought him. At least I think I would. Rattled his keys and marched off.

My cellmate began to stir. A series of groans, then he began to carefully sit up. Alcohol reeked from his pores. He was in his late forties, with receding hairline, a ruddy face and slight build. Wearing jeans and a sweatshirt. All Calvin Klein labels. I'd noticed when I had to turn him. He gingerly raised his head, and I could tell it hurt. He asked,

"Who are you?"

"Jack Taylor."

"Are you my solicitor?"

"No."

He shuffled his body, trying to find a position that didn't ache, then,

"You've a suit . . . are you here to talk to me?"

"No . . . I'm nicked like you."

"Oh."

I waited a bit, asked,

"What would help?"

"Help?"

"Yes, right now . . . what do you need?"

"A drink."

"OK."

Offered the bottle. He stared in jaw-dropping amazement, said,

"It's a trick."

"No, it's Paddy."

A fit of the shakes walloped him. I found an empty cup, poured a small amount in, said,

"Use both hands."

He did. Managed to get it in his mouth, then near convulsed as the liquid went down. I said,

"Wait and see if you're going to be sick. Sometimes the first makes you sick enough so that the second can stay."

He nodded as rivers of sweat broke out on his face. A few minutes and the storm passed. I could see the physical change as his body grasped at the treacherous help. He held out the cup, only a slight tremor, asked,

"May I?"

"Take it easy. This has to get us through the night."

Poured him another, asked,
"Cig?"
Shook his head in wonder, said,
"Jesus, who are you?"
"Nobody . . . a nobody in deep shit."
"Me, too."

THE MAGDALEN

During the endless sessions of rosaries and prayers at the Magdalen, in the days before it finally closed, the girls thought of but one thing: they thought of a day when they'd be able to have a space to breathe and associate beads with something other than punishment. When they finally left the laundry, the deliverance never truly came as, to a person, for the rest of their days, they'd link the rosary to torture.

His accent was Dublin. I'd done enough duty there to know it. I said,

"Southside?"

"Yes . . . are you a Dub?"

"No."

He mopped at his brow, said,

"It's my first time in Galway."

"How do you like it so far?"

He smiled, more due to the cure than anything else, said,

"I'm Danny Flynn."

"So . . . what did you do, Danny?"

A bewildered light in his eyes, he said,

"I don't know. I came down for a stag night . . . in Quay Street . . . you know?"

"I know it."

"Jeez, I'm forty-six, I'm too old for stag parties, too old for this."

I brought out the sandwiches, said,

"Feel up to some food?"

"What you've got there . . . a shop? No thanks. I haven't

eaten for days. I remember going into Freeney's. I can remember the name and then . . . zip. I've had blackouts before. You know what they are?"

"Oh, yeah. I've lost some years myself."

"I've tried all the ways to stop. I go for a time on the dry, then bang."

He said,

"I could manage a cigarette now."

How could I let it slide, said,

"That's the beast . . . accuse it of malice."

I gave him the cigarette, the lighter, and he said,

"Yeah, fucking right."

I yawned and said,

"I'm going to see if I can grab a few hours. Why don't you try, too."

I passed over the bottle, said,

"Take it slow, maybe sneak up on sleep."

"Thanks, Jack."

I lay on my back, fatigue flowing over me. I was about to nod off when,

"Jack?"

"Yeah."

"This is going to sound strange."

"I can do strange."

He gave a laugh, said,

"I'm not sure I can say it right."

"Just spit it out. Nobody here keeping score."

"OK, here goes. I feel safe, isn't that nuts? I mean, I'm in jail, with a stranger, facing God knows what trouble, but I don't have the sense of dread that I usually have."

"Probably the whiskey."

"No, booze makes me numb. Not numb enough to cancel the fear, alas. Here, the last hour or so, I'm OK."

"Enjoy it."

"What?"

"If you have some peace, grab it for all it's worth. My trouble has always been, if I got some grace, I analysed it to death."

"I'll do that. Good night, Jack."

"Yeah."

Much more and we'd have sounded like a jailhouse *Waltons*.

I was woken by the cell door being unlocked by a guard with a tray; took me a minute to orientate. Not that I think you can ever do that in a cell. It's going to be a constant shock. He said,

"Court at nine."

I nodded. On the tray were tea, porridge and toast. Could be worse. I tried some, then it dawned on me.

Where was Danny's tray? Where was Danny?

His bunk was rolled up, no sign of occupancy. How early had they moved him, and why hadn't he woken me? I looked under my pillow. The whiskey was there and half full. Checked my pockets, found the cigarettes and lighter. I couldn't figure it, but this was my first jail time, how much could I know?

When the guard came back, I asked,

"What happened to Danny?"

"Who?"

I indicated his bunk, said,

"The other guy . . . he's from Dublin."

He stared at me, asked,

"Are you in the jigs?"

"No, I'm serious. He was here. Maybe you weren't on duty."

He continued to stare, then,

"I don't know what your problem is. You've had the cell to yourself. In the book, it's down as single occupancy."

Then a bitter laugh.

"If it was the weekend, you'd be jammed to the rafters."

I let it go. So they were fucking with my head, had to be. I recalled the priest, Fr Tom, at the cathedral. The nun telling me, there was no such person. Was this a similar deal, my mind finally gone? Played it over and over till two guards appeared, said,

"Time to go."

I didn't mention Danny.

I'd expected to be brought in the prison van. They used the squad car. The court was busy. Barristers, guards, clerks milling about. I was brought into the court, placed beside a line of subdued men. Ages ranged from late teens to me. Nobody spoke and there was no sense of brothers in adversity. A man detached himself from the other side of the room, strolled over. He had to be a barrister; it leaked from him. He leaned over the rail, asked,

"Jack Taylor?"

I nodded, and he said,

"Brian Casey. I'm representing you."

Before I could answer, the judge entered and proceedings began. I was number three on the docket. When I was called, the judge listened to the charge.

"Assault and battery. Wilful destruction of public property. Reckless endangerment."

The guards objected to bail. Hearing that, my stomach churned. The thought of not getting out was terrifying. My barrister squared up, said,

"My client is well known in the community, with deep roots

and ties to his home town. He has been mentioned many times in the local press for his service to the city."

He droned on about my outstanding character. I had no idea who he was talking about.

The judge finally cut him off, set a trial date for three months hence and granted bail on a large warranty. Then he called,

"Next."

Carey came over, all smiles, said,

"That's it."

"But the bail?"

"I've been instructed to take care of that. Off you go. I'll be in touch."

I had a ton of questions but most wanted to get the hell away from there. I couldn't believe I was actually free. Outside the courthouse, I lit a cig, my hands trembling. Began to move down the steps, heard,

"Morning, Jack."

Leaning against one of the pillars was Kirsten. Dressed in a navy blue power suit. Dressed for business. She walked towards me, said,

"Come on, I'll buy you breakfast."

All my previous resolutions vanished. A night in jail makes you grab for any warmth, and she sure sounded warm. I said,

"Sure."

Went to a new place in Woodquay. The owner was Italian, seemed thrilled to see us, went,

"Buon giorno."

Kirsten grimaced, said,

"Whatever."

He ushered us to a window table, beamed,

"Watch the world go by."

Kirsten touched my hand, said,

"You'll need something substantial."

"Bail was substantial enough."

She turned to the man, said,

"Espresso, twice."

Then she released my hand, asked,

"Was it . . . what's the term . . . hard time?"

"I think I hallucinated."

"Wonderful. See anything interesting?"

As if I'd been to the movies, I said,

"What it was, was sad."

"Did you mark the days off on the wall, pin up girlie photos?"

"You arranged the lawyer?"

"And bail."

"I owe you."

She ran her hand through her hair, then,

"You owe me big time."

No denying that.

The coffee came. She took a sip, said,

"Mmmmm, authentic."

I reached for my cigs, and she said,

"Light two."

"You're smoking now?"

"I like to revisit all my vices."

She took one drag, stubbed it out, said,

"The guy you hit, I know him."

"Oh."

"A little pressure and he could be persuaded to drop the charges."

"I doubt if he will."

She tilted her head, said,

"You really don't understand how things work, do you, Jack?"

"Probably not."

She tapped a fingernail against her cup. Light enamel on the nail caught the reflection from the window. She asked,

"You know what a cluster fuck is, Jack?"

As before, the ease with which she swore took me blindside. I had to wait a moment before I answered.

"I could take a guess."

"I thought you might. In case you're not sure, it's what you get when you piss off a group of powerful people. You seem to have a knack of doing that. Tourism is a vital part of our city's income, and if you dredge up past shame, you throw a shadow over the whole deal."

I drank some of the coffee. She was right, it was great. I asked,

"How did you know I was in jail?"

"The grapevine. I thought you'd need help."

"Let me see if I have it right. If I drop certain investigations . . . the Magdalen, yours . . . I'll be all right."

She gave her radiant smile.

"Exactly."

I stood, said,

"Thanks for the coffee."

"You can't ascribe our fall from grace to any single event or set of circumstances. You can't lose what you lacked at conception. It's time to demythologise an era and build a new myth from the gutter to the stars."

James Ellroy, *American Tabloid*

As I left the café, the owner said,

"*Ciao.*"

I didn't answer him. It wasn't my day for fostering European unity. As I walked up Eyre Street, coming to Roches, I didn't meet a soul I knew. Not that there weren't people. The paths were crowded. Galway had become a city. As a child, if I walked down the town, I knew every single person. Not only that, I knew all belonging to them.

Part of me welcomed the new anonymity, but I felt something had been lost. Not so much familiarity, more a comforting intimacy. Finally a man said,

"Jack?"

A guy I'd gone to school with. Jeez, how long ago was that? I guessed,

"Sean?"

It must have been correct, as he shook my hand, said,

"The last time I saw you, you were going to be a guard."

I was tempted to say,

"And you had hair . . . teeth."

But he was friendly, and that was vital right then. I asked,

"How have you been?"

He considered, then,

"I was in hospital."

"Oh."

"It's full of non-nationals."

"What have they got?"

"Mainly medical cards."

I smiled at the casual racism. He wasn't sure which side of a liberal fence I was on, so he ventured,

"Beds are scarce. You leave it, you lose it."

"And now . . . how are you?"

"Middling."

This is a classic Irish answer. It shows they're not complaining, yet leaves the door open for any sympathy that might be on offer. He studied me, asked,

"What happened to the suit?"

I checked the tear, which seemed to have grown, said,

"A difference of opinion."

He gave the mandatory expression of pain, said,

"They took out my stomach last year."

"They" could be . . . muggers, passers-by, doctors.

I nodded as if it made any sense. He said,

"You know what's the hardest thing?"

God knows, various answers came, but I decided not to run with them. Instead,

"I don't."

"Chips and chocolate. I was a hoor for them."

"They're a loss."

"Fierce. I could murder a plate of chips and vinegar, then the king size bar of milk chocolate."

He looked totally desolate, then,

"Course I have my prayers."

"You do?"

"I'd be lost without them."

He looked toward the Square, said,

"There's my bus."

"You take care."

"I will, Jack. Eat a bag of chips for me."

As I watched him walk away, I felt a yearning for a simpler era. Not that I'd ever keep it simple. No matter how plain sailing it might have got, I'd manage to complicate it. Alcoholics patented the concept of snatching defeat from any glimmer of victory. Lit a cig, and a passing woman said,

"Them yokes will kill you."

"They'll have to stand in line."

*"What I would call a supernatural and mystical experience has in its very essence
some note of a direct spiritual contact of two liberties, a kind of flash or spark
which ignites an intuition . . . plus something much more which I can only
describe as personal in which God is known not as an object or as 'Him up there'
but as the biblical expression, I am . . . this is not the kind of intuition
that smacks of anything procurable because it is a presence of a Person and
depends on the liberty of the person."*

Thomas Merton in a letter to Aldous Huxley

When I got to the hotel, Mrs Bailey came out from reception,
said,

"You've been in the wars."

"I have."

"Give me that jacket, I'll put a stitch in."

"There's no need."

"And what, you're going to walk around like a vagrant?"

It was easier to concede. I took the jacket off, handed it over.
She examined the cloth, tut-tutted, said,

"They get away with murder."

I left her muttering. Upstairs, I went straight to my stash, got
two heavy duty pills, took them fast. I wanted a shower so bad
I could scream. First, I rummaged round, found the ban garda's
number, dialled. A few minutes, then,

"Hello?"

"Ridge, it's Jack Taylor."

"Oh, I didn't expect you to call."

"Me either. You said you wanted to help."

"I do."

"OK. Run background on Mrs Kirsten Boyle. Lives in Taylor's Hill. Her husband died recently."

"What do you want to know?"

"Who she is."

"I'll see what I can find out."

Click.

Jeez, she was a tough girl to like. I lay back on the bed, thought,

"I'll grab that shower in a minute."

Slept until late evening. My dreams were vivid. Saw my father with his head hung in shame. Saw the love of my life, Ann Henderson, walking away and heard Danny Flynn say,

"I'm safe."

Like I said . . . vivid.

*"I just wish, though, that the human race was not quite
so often trapped by its own versatility."*

John Arden, Introduction to *Cogs Tyrannic*

It took me two days to find Bill Cassell. His usual haunt,
Sweeney's, remained closed. I trawled through Galway's late
night pubs, hearing a word here, a hint there. He was not somebody people were comfortable talking about.

Since Casey, his bodyguard, was shot, he hadn't been seen either. Now I learnt he was in Belfast, having his knee rebuilt.
The experts in such injuries are there. If you want information
and fast, pay for it,

I did.

Found lots of information, including a special piece of Bill's
family history that I knew I could use to manipulate him. I never
expected to find this; it just turned up in my search.

Tracked down the barman who'd tended Sweeney's. He was
a bouncer at a club in Eglington Street. When I finally caught
up with him, he was on his break, having a drink at the bar. I
said,

"How you doing?"

"Fuck off."

"You know me?"

He didn't even look at me, said,

"I don't care who you are, fuck off."

"Want some money?"

Now he looked, said,

"Taylor . . . yeah, I remember you."

"So, do you want the money or not?"

"What do I have to do?"

"Tell me where Bill Cassell is."

I showed him the wad of money. He drained his glass, belched, then massaged his beer gut, said,

"Sure, I can tell you."

"Go ahead."

"Bill's in the hospice. The cancer is in the last stages. Old Bill won't be coming back."

I handed over the money, said,

"You don't sound too sorry."

"For him? Good fucking riddance. His strong arm guy, he got shot in the knee."

"Who shot him?"

"Some fuck with a bad aim."

"Bad?"

"Yeah, he should have blown his head off."

He stood up, said,

"I have to go back to work, crack some skulls."

I went to the hospice early in the morning. Had rung first to confirm he was there and to establish visiting hours. You'd expect it to be a dark, depressing place.

It wasn't.

Full of light, bright colours and warm, cheerful staff. When I asked at reception for Bill, the woman smiled, said,

"You're here to visit?"

"Yes."

"Follow me."

I was carrying flowers, chocolates, fruit and lucozade: all the ingredients of bad karma. We stopped at a bright blue door and she knocked. We heard,

"Come in."

She said,

"I'll leave you to surprise him."

"I intend to."

I opened the door. At first I couldn't see him, then realised it was because he'd wasted away to such a degree. His head propped on the pillow was almost transparent. The eyes retained their ferocity.

Wilde said,

"Put a man in a mask, and he'll tell you the truth."

I was hoping a hospital bed might have the same effect. I crossed the room, moved the wastebasket with my foot, let the goodies crash into it, said,

"What, you thought that I brought them for you?"

Moved right up to him, caught the front of his pyjamas in my left hand. He weighed nothing. With my right fist, I punched him twice in the side of his head.

Hard solid blows.

The ferocity slipped from his eyes to be replaced by shock. I doubt if any one had ever touched him in his adult life. I let go and he fell back. I pulled up a chair, took out my cigs, said,

"Don't suppose they like smoking?"

Lit up.

Gradually, his focus returned, and I said,

"Tell me about Rita Monroe."

His breath came in laboured gasps as he began,

"She was the bitch from hell. Delighted in tormenting the

Magdalen girls. Used to make my mother stand outside wrapped in wet sheets. Shaved their hair off, plus the daily beatings and starvation. Her favourite trick was to stand my mother in boiling water to burn the evil out!"

"Who killed her nephews?"

He gave a tight smile,

"How would I know? But if you wanted to torture somebody, really make them suffer, then take away what they love most. She'd no family, but I hear she adored those boys. I had hoped to meet her face to face, ask her how it felt."

He indicated his situation, said,

"As you can see, I'm otherwise engaged."

"You turned my room over?"

"Me? . . . though I hear you're still at Bailey's."

"And the break-ins at her house?"

"Again, I wouldn't know. I like the suggestion, get her nice and shaky for the main event."

I pushed the chair back. He didn't flinch, said,

"What? You're going to beat me to death. You'd be doing me a favour. Another week, I'll be dead anyway. You wonder why I employed you? You see, I needed a witness. I could have found that cunt any time. You see how easy it was to locate the nephews, but you had to be convinced it was a genuine search, otherwise what sort of witness would you have made? I wanted her to feel safe, secure, thinking the past was done. But once my own time was measured, it was get the game in motion. I used you to fuck with you. Your room was trashed as a little extra, as I know how precious those bloody books were to you. Did it piss you off, get your motor running? I always hated you, swaggering round as a guard, like you were something special. Getting you involved, how much of a swagger have you now?"

I looked at him, said,

"You hired me because you knew I'd find her, though?"

"Course. It made you an accomplice."

"Well then, Bill, you won't be surprised to know I found somebody else."

He attempted to sit up, apprehension on his face. I said,

"I thought about our schooldays, what I knew about you, then I remembered: you had a sister."

Spittle forming at the corners of his mouth, he rasped,

"You leave her out of this. It's nothing to do with her."

I had his full attention, said,

"Maggie. Quiet girl, never married and . . ."

I paused, as if I wanted to arrange the information in my head, then,

"Lives alone at 14 Salthill Avenue. No visible means of support. You take care of her, don't you?"

"So what?"

"So, I'd like you to think over this for the next week."

"You stay away from her, hear me."

"Imagine, Bill, a delicate person like that, how they'd react to a campaign of harassment and intimidation. I don't need to tell you how easy it is to frighten a woman alone."

Rage tore at his wasted body. He asked,

"What do you want?"

"Jeez, Bill, I don't want anything. I don't think Maggie's going to do very well when you're gone."

"I'll tell you who the shooter is."

"OK."

He closed his eyes, the struggle not to concede stretched across his forehead, then,

"Michael Neville. He has one of those flats beside the Spanish Arch. On the top floor. There's something wrong with him, apart from the fact that he endlessly chews Juicy Fruit. He's not really there; it's like he's imitating a person but not making much of an effort."

I moved to go, and he asked,

"That's it?"

"Yes."

"You'll leave her alone . . . Maggie . . . she's not like us . . . she . . ."

"Well, Bill, I'll think about it."

I opened the door, and he shouted,

"Jesus, Jack, come back. Give me some guarantee."

I closed the door, began to walk up the corridor. Met the receptionist, who asked,

"Did the visit go well?"

"It did."

"He'll be easier in himself then."

"I'd say so."

"You were good to come."

"He and I go back a long way."

She digested that, searched for a cliché to fit, said,

"Old friends are the best ones."

"I couldn't have put it better myself."

As I came out to the main road, a bus was approaching. It would have taken me all the way to the city centre. I decided to walk. Passed a phone kiosk and thought,

"Two minutes, I could ring the guards, tell them what I know, and Michael Neville would be picked up in no time. Plus, I'd maybe score myself some points with Clancy."

Kept walking.

Or, I could call the ban garda, let her get the glory.

No, this was something I had to do alone. When I got to the top of Bohermore, I crossed the road. Stood outside the gates of the cemetery. I wanted to enter, visit Brendan's grave, pay some respect. My feet wouldn't move.

Took out a cigarette and muttered,

"Come on, it's no big thing. Walk in, find the grave, say hello, and you're out of there."

Couldn't do it.

Part of it was how he'd have reacted to my treatment of Bill. Could hear him go,

"You did what? Went into a dying man's room, beat him in the bed?"

As bare as that, sure sounded rough. I'd try to rally with,

"He was a piece of shit, garbage. He had two innocent young men murdered, terrorised a frail old woman."

He'd shake his head.

"God forgive you, because no one else will."

And if I were desperate enough, I'd try,

"But I got results, didn't I? The case is solved."

"It's not right, Jack. You know it's not."

A gravedigger came out of the gate. Another guy from my schooldays, he was carrying a thermos and sandwiches, said,

"Jack, you're talking to yourself."

"Bad sign, isn't it?"

"Ah, don't worry about it. I talk to myself all the time."

He saw me eye his lunch, said,

"Most days I eat in there."

Nodding back towards the cemetery, continued,

"But times, I need to get out, be in the flow of people."

I could understand that, said,

"I can understand that."

"No, it's not like you think. The peace is indescribable, but I'll be long enough there eventually. So I force myself to circulate."

I decided not to visit, said,

"Good to talk to you."

"You know where I am, where we'll all be. The calendar solves everything."

I stood outside the apartment building at the Spanish Arch. Bill said Michael Neville lived on the top floor. I checked the names on the outside. Sure enough, there he was, 5A. I rang the number. No answer. If he'd answered, I'm not sure what I'd have said. I kept hoping some sophisticated plan would strike me.

None did.

In the movies, to gain entrance, the hero rings one of the other tenants and they always let him in.

Didn't work.

I decided to put my garda training to use. I forced the lock. Not easily or even quietly. Pure brute strength. In the hall, I found the stairs and began to climb. On the fifth floor, I stood outside 5A, listened. No sound of activity. Knocked on the door and heard,

"Yeah?"

"ESB."

"Just a minute."

Adrenaline was pumping along my veins. Then the rattle of a dead bolt and the locks being turned, and the door opened.

A man in a vest and boxer shorts stood there. He was wiping sleep from his eyes. I asked,

"Michael Neville?"

"Yes."

I punched him in the stomach. Then followed with another to his chin. He fell back inside. I checked the corridor then stepped over him. Dragged him to the living room and shut the door. He was early thirties, thin and not difficult to haul. I quickly checked the other rooms for occupancy.

If he had company, I was fucked. He didn't. I searched the bedroom, found a Browning automatic and my own gun. In a shoebox were a stash of cocaine and a large amount of money. Put the coke, money and HK in my jacket. Kept the Browning in my hand. Could hear him groaning as he began to regain consciousness.

I went back to the living room, pulled a chair up and sat over him. I let the gun rest lightly on my knee. His eyes opened and he sat up, massaging his jaw. I said,

"Hi."

He stared at me, said,

"Taylor! I told Bill we should have done you. Get a chance to rent the video of *The Deer Hunter*?"

He tried to stand, and I said,

"Bad idea unless you want me to shoot your toes off."

Alongside me, I noticed a book. I was so surprised he'd have one that I picked it up. You just don't associate hit men with reading. The title was *Doting*.

I said,

"Hey, nobody reads Henry Green any more."

He stared at me in confusion, asked,

"What are you talking about?"

I was allowing my concentration to slip. I can't blame books for the chaos of my life, but they've always been there on the journey. I said,

"He's a famously neglected writer. He gets rediscovered every decade or so."

He was almost standing now. I continued,

"He wrote nothing for the last twenty years of his life."

Neville said,

"It isn't mine. Was in the apartment when I came. Was going to sling it, but you never know. I run out of toilet paper, I'll use that."

A sort of madness in myself. I was determined he'd know about this author. I said,

"He never let his photo be taken, used the pseudonym and gave interviews that revealed little. Critics described his work as elusive and enigmatic. In fact, very similar to the characteristics of your own work."

He was standing now, said,

"Fuck you."

I moved the book towards him, said,

"His real name was Henry Vincent Yorke. Born in Tewkesbury, England. Served in the Auxiliary Fire Service during the Second World War. After, he returned to his family's firm in the Midlands, wrote in his spare time."

Neville had moved closer, said,

"You're a fucking whacko, you know that? You've made a serious mistake, but tell you what: give me the gun, you get to walk out of here."

I watched him, saw his muscles tense, said,

"You don't want to know about Henry, do you? That he wrote ten novels. Listen, sometimes you hear about 'a writer's writer'. Well, he's been described as 'the writer's writer's writer'."

He lunged for me. As I fell backward, the gun went off. Didn't even sound like a shot, more of a muted pop. I was on the ground, Neville across me. He wasn't moving. I shoved him and he rolled over, his eyes blank. A small hole in his chest. If I'd been aiming, I'd never have achieved such a result.

I moved to the door, listened, but heard nothing. Went back to Neville, checked his pulse. There was none. I took the coke out, did two lines to steady myself, then systematically began to wipe down anything I'd touched. There was a huge array of Juicy Fruit on the floor and I let it lie. As the coke racked my brain, I went over every surface again. Could feel the ice dribble down the back of my throat, the euphoria and the physical well-being from the drug. I poured the remainder of the white powder over his body. There was an envelope with his name and address, which I put in my pocket. I hoped the cocaine might influence the guards' investigation.

I looked at his body, thought,

"I know absolutely nothing about you."

I put the still warm gun in my jacket. Took a glance around, hoped I hadn't overlooked anything. Opened the door, no one in the corridor. Down the stairs, the coke shooting along my nerves. If I met one person, I was finished. At the front door, I stepped outside, kept my head low. Within minutes I was at Jury's Hotel and risked a look back. The apartment building seemed the same. No squealing police cars or alarmed citizens.

I tried to tell myself,

"Christ, you've been lucky."

It's a little hard to mention luck when a man was lying on a floor with a bullet in his heart.

Moved off towards Quay Street. Turned left and walked into Kirwan's Lane.

"But I wouldn't kill anybody for money. No matter how much I needed it. I'm not the man for it. My memory is too good. I wouldn't want to relive over and over the sight of some poor fool going down under the weight of his own blood."

John Straley, *Death and the Language of Happiness*

Kirwan's Lane is regarded as Galway's most important medieval passage. The Kirwans were one of the twelve tribes who founded the city. There's a small theatre there where Wolfe Tone appeared. It was begun by a man with the wonderful name Humanity Dick Martin.

I could hear music coming from Busker Brown's. This pub includes part of the "Slate Nunnery", a building presented to the Dominican nuns in 1686 by John Kirwan. It was to become the first convent of the Presentation nuns.

I didn't know what put all that in my head. The only history I obsess with is my own.

Maybe I thought I could use it to erase the present.

Some chance.

I did know I badly needed to talk to someone. Found a phone kiosk that hadn't been vandalised and rang Nestor's. Jeff answered. I said,

"It's Jack, are you busy now?"

"No."

"Could we meet somewhere?"

"Sure."

We met in a coffee shop on Quay Street. He said,

"I never get down this side of town."

"This is where it all happens."

"That's why I don't get down here."

He looked like a biker. Beat-up Harley jacket, Jethro Tull sweatshirt, black cords and heavy boots. I said,

"That's retro."

He gave an easy smile, said,

"I was going to take the Soft Tail out to Clifden, just open her up, feel the surge."

Clifden had very bad memories for me. Before they could grip, Jeff asked,

"What's on your mind? You don't look so good."

I took a breath, said,

"Recently, two people I met, a priest and . . . a drinker . . . Well, I don't know how to put this, but they seem not to have been real."

He didn't appear fazed, thought about it, asked,

"Tell me about them."

"How do you mean?"

"The kind of people they were, what you felt about them."

So I described the meeting with Fr Tom and then the encounter with Danny. If he was surprised by my night in jail, he was keeping it under wraps. He said,

"Let me see if I got this right. You were comfortable, could talk easily with them."

"Yes."

Then he gave me a studied look, said,

"At a guess, you're doing 'ludes, beauties, some other heavy downers and still pouring the booze in. Am I right?"

I felt exposed, vulnerable, and couldn't find an answer. He said,

"Jack, I was in a band, remember? I've done all the trips and I sure recognise the signs."

"You think I'm losing it?"

"I think it's predicable that usage like yours brings some vivid hallucinations."

"I'm tripping out?"

"It's interesting that those people didn't threaten or condemn you. In a perverse way, they're like manifestations of your personality."

"I'm fucked."

"Jack, pay attention. You're under some heavy stress, and your unconscious provided friends you could relate to."

"What am I going to do?"

"Get off the drugs."

"Jesus."

We sat in silence for a time, then he asked,

"What's going to happen with your assault charge?"

"I've got a lawyer."

He smiled, said,

"Sounds like you're going to need one."

I gave him the background as to why I'd hit the guy, let him digest it, then asked,

"If you'd been me, Jeff, would you have done any different?"

"I don't know, Jack. I'd like to think I'd have intervened, but I'd probably have walked by."

The café was beginning to fill up, so we headed out. Walked towards Shop Street. I said,

"I appreciate you taking the time, Jeff."

"I'm your friend, you should call me more often."

Back at the hotel, I sat on my bed and wondered if I should just head for London. Toyed with that but couldn't get it to fly. Laid the guns in the bed, thought,

"I'm armed to the teeth."

I knew I should ditch the Browning. When the body of Neville was found, they'd have the bullet. How hard was it going to be to tell the type of weapon it came from? If they ever got the gun, it would be game, set and match.

I decided to hold on to it. I held the envelope with Michael Neville's name and address and wondered why I'd taken that, more incriminating evidence. I put it with the gun and stashed them.

It was three days before they found the body. At first the reports said only that a man had been found dead in a city centre apartment. Then later, that the police were treating it as suspicious.

Bullet holes do that.

Finally, a full-scale murder inquiry was launched. The guards were said to be following a definite line of inquiry. A spokesman said,

"We will not allow drug trafficking to escalate in the city."

I could breathe, if not easily, at least without constriction.

My barrister summoned me.

His offices were on Mainguard Street. Up two flights of
stairs, past a receptionist and into his den. His certificates were
framed along the wall. We both admired them for a moment,
then he said,

"Right, Mr Taylor, I have some encouraging news."

"Great."

"It's possible the case will be dropped."

"Why?"

"The . . . *victim* . . . not that we'd ever use such a term outside this office . . . am I right?"

I had no argument there, said,

"You won't hear me calling him a victim."

"Capital, that's the ticket. You've just learnt a whole chunk
about the law."

He was wearing a suit that quietly proclaimed,

"I'm a winner

You . . . most definitely

Are not."

He flicked through some pages, said,

"Now, the guards may press ahead on the criminal damages."

"Oh."

He waved a hand in dismissal.

"They're just making noise, letting us know they're on the job. If you're willing to pay compensation, I can make it go away."

He paused, adopted a sterner tone, said,

"You are willing to do that?"

"Of course."

"Good man. I'll get that attended to right away. Looks better if you've paid before the case gets called. Shows you're contrite . . . and you are . . . aren't you, Mr Taylor?"

"Completely."

"Okey-dokey, that covers it. I'll be in touch as soon as I have further information. My nose tells me you won't have to even appear in court."

"That's amazing."

He leaned back in his swivel chair, said,

"No, it's expediency."

"What about your fees?"

"None of your concern you'll be happy to hear."

"Why?"

"Let's say I'm glad to be in a position to accommodate Kirsten."

We both were aware of his use of her first name. I let that linger, then said,

"Thank you."

"Mr Taylor?"

"Yes."

"Don't depend on expediency in the future. It's not on-going."

I'd reached the door when he added,

"You wouldn't want to fall foul of the people who've helped you."

"Gee, that sounds a lot like a threat."

He raised his eyebrows, exclaimed,

"I'm in the legal profession. I don't make threats."

"You're kidding. You never do anything else. The only difference is you have certificates for it."

I'd cut down on the pills. Instead of the usual two for breakfast, I held out till noon and took one. Called it maintenance. Cold turkey was the last thing I could face. I headed back for the hotel, wondering why I didn't feel relieved at the solicitor's news. It looked like I wasn't going to jail, but I knew I wasn't off the hook. Somebody was going to expect payback.

In the lobby, Mrs Bailey said,

"There's a young man to see you."

"Oh."

"He's waiting in the lounge."

"Right."

"Mr Taylor, he seems a very angry young man."

"Aren't they all?"

It was Terry Boyle. In an expensive suit, not unlike the solicitor's; definitely in the same price range, a level that remained forever beyond me. He was, as they say, spitting iron. I said,

"Terry."

He was shaking from temper, snarled,

"You're shagging Kirsten."

"Whoa . . . keep your voice down."

"I will not."

I raised my hand. He stepped back, and I said,

"OK, now let's sit down and you can try and cool off."

We did.

I took out my cigs, fired up. He waved at the smoke, said,

"I hired you, and what do you do? You bloody go to bed with the bitch."

"Who told you that?"

"She did."

"And you believed her?"

It was if he'd been waiting for such an answer, asked,

"Do you have a tattoo of an angel on your chest?"

"I . . ."

"You do . . . Jesus . . . let me see."

Grabbed at my shirt, tore the buttons. I caught his wrist, said,

"Over the past week, I've punched out three people. The thing is, I'm developing a taste for it. Here's what you have to ask yourself. Do you want your wrist broken?"

I bent it towards the floor, and he said,

"All right . . . God, you're so physical."

"Are you going to behave, because you're all out of warnings?"

He pulled back from me, massaged his wrist, moaned,

"That hurt."

I tried to arrange my ruined shirt, said,

"I liked that shirt. You have no idea how fast I'm getting through wardrobes."

His lip curled, actually turned up at the right corner, and he said,

"Sartorial is a description that would not readily spring to mind about you. One feels the charity shops have all your requirements."

He was the kind of guy you'd never tire of beating the bejaysus out of. I said,

"Terry, I've checked out Kirsten. No matter how much you detest her, there's no proof she killed your father."

"And, of course, you investigated fully, especially in his bed. No clues there I suppose, or were you too preoccupied?"

"Give it up, Terry. It's a waste of time."

He jumped to his feet, said,

"I'm meeting her next week. One way or another, I'll sort the tramp."

"Come on, Terry."

"Fuck you, Jack Taylor. You're a despicable human being."

And he was gone.

Mrs Bailey came over, asked,

"Can I get you something?"

"No . . . thank you."

"The young man, were you able to help him?"

"I don't think so."

"If you don't mind me saying so, Mr Taylor, storm clouds appear to be constantly over you."

"You got that right."

THE MAGDALEN

The day Lucifer left the laundry, she got up early, packed her small suitcase and gazed at the items of jewellery she had. Two small Claddagh rings, a pearl rosary and a small gold cross on a silver chain. These had belonged to "the Martyrs", the girls whose deaths she had caused. Fingering the cross, she considered bringing it to the pawn on Quay Street, but it gave her such a thrill of remembrance, the surge of power she'd felt when those girls died. With a sigh, she put the cross in her bag, decided to keep it as a reminder of these glory days.

There would never be another time like this, and she knew her life would only be downhill after this. Her sister had two sons, and Lucifer adored them. She'd thanked the dark power she worshipped that her sister hadn't had girls. After her time at the Magdalen, her hatred of women was even more entrenched, because they were so weak, always whining, always conspiring. A small laugh escaped her as she thought, "I sure put manners on the little cows. They won't forget me in a hurry."

I went upstairs, took off the torn shirt. Examined it in the vague hope of salvage, but it was beyond help. Slung it in the bin. The phone went. I picked it up, said,

"Yes?"

"Jack . . . it's Bríd . . . Bríd Nic an Iomaire."

"Ridge."

Could hear her annoyance, then she said,

"I got the information you wanted."

"On Kirsten?"

"Yes."

"Good girl."

"Don't be so condescending."

"Good woman?"

"I'll be in McSwiggan's at eight."

Click.

I began to listen to the death notices. How fucked is that? Instead of my morning drugs, I'd listen for those. Mental abuse of a whole different calibre. A lot of the names had a ring of familiarity. I was in that age range where you no longer watch for the success of your friends; you await news of their demise.

Then,

"Bill Cassell."

As I rushed to turn the volume up, I noted the removal arrangements and

"No flowers by request. All donations to Galway Hospice."

I didn't know if that was a funeral I'd attend. It was due to leave the Augustinian at eleven the next day. If for no other reason, I should go to ensure he was truly gone.

That evening, I wore a sweatshirt, jeans and my guards coat. Despite the burning, it was still intact. I got to McSwiggan's at eight fifteen. Ridge was already there, toying with a bottle of Diet Coke. I asked,

"Get you another?"

"No."

I ordered a double Jameson; felt I'd been doing well with my cutback on the pills. I sat opposite her, said,

"We're almost a regular feature here."

No smile, no reply. She was wearing a white T-shirt, navy jeans. Her face was without makeup, and it made her look severe, aloof. Reaching in her bag, she took out a notebook, said,

"Interesting person, this Kirsten Boyle."

"That's one way of describing her."

She gave me a full stare, asked,

"Are you involved with her?"

"Not in that way."

"Well, it's what she does, collect men."

I didn't comment so she began:

"Her real name is Mary Cowan. From Waterford, lower middle class background, regular upbringing, nothing out of the ordinary. At sixteen, she met a rich English guy, ran off to England with him."

"No crime there."

"Ten years later, she arrives in Galway, with a new name, new accent and a recently deceased husband."

"Oh."

"Five years ago, she married again and became Mrs Boyle. Before and since the death of Boyle, she's had a string of men. Her husband died of a heart attack; he was cremated quickly. Obviously, she has friends who expedite such matters. Normally there'd be a post mortem."

I repeated,

"Expedite."

"What?"

"It's a word that appears to cling to her."

"What clings to her is influence. She knows the right people."

"You've got that right."

She took a sip of the Coke, asked,

"Why are you interested in her?"

"I was asked to check her out."

"You're investigating her . . . no, no . . . you're investigating the death of her husband."

When I didn't answer, she said,

"There's nothing to prove she did anything."

I asked,

"How did you discover so much?"

"My Uncle Brendan taught me well. His favourite line was, 'It's not what you know but knowing where the information lies.' "

I said,

"He sure would have been proud of you."

A pained expression lit her face, then was replaced by the severe look. She said,

"I am so angry with him."

I nodded, and she snapped,

"With you, too."

"Me?"

"You were his friend, weren't you?"

"Um . . . yes."

"Why didn't you watch out for him?"

"I wasn't focused . . ."

She stood up, near spat,

"And when are you focused? When you're ordering large whiskies, is that when you pay attention? You were a poor excuse for a friend."

After she'd left, I remembered what Babs Simpson had once said,

"Alcoholics are almost always charming. They have to be, because they have to keep making new friends. They use up the old ones."

She'd been the editor of *Vogue* and *Harper's Bazaar*.

Her indictment had seared my soul. I don't even think she meant it as such. If anything, she'd said it with a knowing resignation.

I don't know how long I sat staring into my glass. All the grief I'd caused and endured had come storming upon my soul. At the very best of times, I was never "fond" of myself. For that moment, I was full of self-loathing. Then, I understood how Brendan could arrange a noose, step on a kitchen chair and swing. A middle-aged woman was cleaning and clearing the tables. I observed without caring a badge in her blouse. One of those frigging smile jobs. Written underneath was,

"Put on a happy face."

I could have happily torn it off and made her eat it. She indicated Ridge's Diet Coke, asked,

"Is that a dead soldier?"

"Oh yes."

She paused, and I knew I was getting her scrutiny. I didn't look up. She said,

"Cheer up, it might never happen."

"It already has."

Stymied her, but not for long. She was the type who'd find merit in politics. She said,

"You never know what's around the corner."

Now I looked up, pinned her with everything I'd been feeling, said,

"If it bears the slightest resemblance to my past, even the tiniest similarity, then I'm fucked."

She took off quick.

Bill Cassell's funeral rates as one of the most miserable I've ever attended. God knows, I've clocked up my quota. They've ranged from upbeat through pathetic to the plain sad. But for sheer misery, this was the pits.

A filthy day, the driving rain that soaks you entirely. No amount of wet gear is sufficient. You feel it dribble down your neck, wash along your legs, saturate your socks. It is relentless, a ferocious cold, and you understand the true meaning of "wretched". Four people in all at the graveside. The priest, Fr Malachy, who had tried to light a cigarette. He failed. A gravedigger and a tiny frail woman. I was the fourth. Malachy rushed through some empty psalm. I helped the gravedigger lower the coffin. He was grunting with effort. I asked,

"Aren't there usually two of you?"

"He wouldn't come out in this weather."

We made a bad job of it. The ropes cut into my hands, and

I broke the nails on two fingers. When we were done, the woman stopped forward, let a single white rose flutter down. I moved to her, asked,

"Maggie?"

"Yes?"

"You're Bill's sister?"

She shrank back from me, as if I was about to assault her. Her whole demeanour was that of a whipped dog. Not only had she the body language of a victim, but also her eyes said she lived in expectation of further punishment. I tried to appear as unthreatening as I could. Not easy when you're bundled in a guard's coat, wet through and two feet from an open grave. She answered,

"Yes."

As if pleading guilty.

I put out my hand, said,

"Jack Taylor."

Her hand met mine slowly and she asked,

"Were you Bill's friend?"

She had huge saucer eyes; guile or badness had never touched them. I didn't want to out and out lie to such a person, so I said,

"We went to school together."

"Bill didn't like school."

"Me neither."

This seemed to ease her apprehension, and she said,

"You were so good to come and it being such a woeful day."

I had no truthful reply. Malachy touched me on the shoulder, asked,

"A word?"

I said to Maggie,

"Excuse me a moment."

And I turned to him, snapped,

"What?"

He backed up. Jesus, everybody was doing that. The vibes coming from me must have been deadly. He said,

"I'm surprised you're here."

"Like it's any of your business."

He made a vain attempt to wipe rain from his face. Even his dog collar was soaked. He said,

"Your mother had a stroke."

"Yeah?"

"Good God, man, is that all you have to say?"

"Where is she?"

"She's back home now. Will you go to see her?"

"I'll think about it."

"You have the heart of the devil."

"Thanks."

I turned back to Maggie. She was gazing at the grave with such a profound look of desolation. I'd have taken her arm but felt she'd have jumped. I said,

"Maggie, can I get you a taxi?"

"No, no, I have a car."

She could see my amazement, said,

"Bill bought it. He bullied me into driving lessons. I wasn't very good and I'd have given up, but you know Bill. He wasn't a man you could go against."

I nodded. Here was something I could certainly bear testament to. She said,

"I didn't know what to do after."

"After?"

"You know, people hire hotels and have something for the mourners, but . . ."

Her distress at the lack of people was palpable, so I said,

"Why don't we go and have a drink, raise a toast to his memory?"

Her clutching at this lifeline was awful. She near cried,

"Would you . . . oh . . . that would be wonderful . . . I'll pay . . . We can talk about Bill . . . and . . ."

My heart sank.

Her car, a Toyota, was outside the gate. As she got behind the wheel, she seemed completely disoriented. Before I could speak, she got it together, and with two false starts, we moved into traffic. She gave a smile of defeat, said,

"I'm not very good at this."

"Don't worry."

I figured I'd do enough for the both of us. We went down Bohermore at a snail's pace. Other motorists raged at us. I suggested,

"Maybe move up into third gear."

"Oh."

As we passed Tonery's, I said,

"Pull in here."

More screaming of tyres as we attempted that. We sideswiped a parked van and ground to a halt. I got out fast, waited in the rain for her. She asked,

"Will the car be all right here?"

At least until the van driver arrived. I said,

"Sure."

The pub has a huge sun lounge at the back. Despite the outside deluge, it was bright and welcoming. The barman nodded, said,

"I'll come over."

We sat and she said,

"This is my treat."

I figured she didn't get to say that very often. When the barman came, she said,

"A small sherry."

I ordered Jameson.

We sat in silence till the drinks came. She didn't seem uncomfortable with that, as if it was what she most experienced. I raised my glass, said,

"To . . . Bill."

And she began to cry.

Not the loud sobbing type. Worse, that deep internal heaving that is horrendous to witness. Tears rolled down her cheeks, plinked into her glass. I stared at the rain.

What I was thinking was some lines of Merton that had struck a chord in my soul:

I kept my eyes closed, more out of apathy than anything else. But anyway, there was no need to open one's eyes to see the visitor, to see death. Death is someone you see very clearly with eyes in the centre of your heart; eyes that do not see by reacting to light, but by reacting to a kind of chill from within the marrow of your heart.

She dried her eyes, said,

"It's lovely here."

"It is."

"I don't get out much."

I searched for some cliché to answer, couldn't find one, asked,

"Did Bill ever talk about a Rita Monroe?"

A shudder ran down her body, then,

"He was obsessed with her."

"Why?"

She took some of the sherry, began,

"Bill adored my mother. But she wasn't . . . well. I think she was very . . . brittle."

She gave a nervous laugh, continued,

"Passed it on to me, I think. Anyway, she was always sick and used . . . to harm herself. Then she'd be in the hospital for a long time. Bill couldn't understand it. He'd fly into rages, blame my father, blame me. When she came home, he'd be so delighted. The few times she was well, he was totally different. On fire with joy. After she died, my father sat us down, told us about her time in the Magdalen, that she'd never recovered. How that woman, Rita Monroe, had singled her out for persecution. Once Bill knew, he was like a man possessed."

She looked at me, asked,

"Do you know about hate, Mr Taylor?"

"Please call me Jack. Yes, I do know about it."

Her eyes bored into mine, and I saw a strength there. She said,

"Yes, I think you do. It became Bill's reason for living. This is strange, but he was never more alive than when he was feeding the hatred. As if electricity had touched him. He never tired of planning revenge. You know what he was most afraid of?"

I couldn't imagine, said,

"No."

"That she'd be dead."

"Oh."

"He wanted her to suffer like our mother did."

I considered briefly telling her what I knew. Before I could decide, she said,

"I hope he didn't find her."

"Didn't you want her to pay for what she did to your mother?"

She shook her head, said,

"If she was so . . . demonic . . . as we're told . . . life itself would deal with her."

I finished my drink, said,

"I'm not so sure I agree with that."

"Mr Taylor, Jack, my brother destroyed his life with hatred and cast a malignant shadow on mine. If he'd found that woman, it wouldn't have made any difference. He'd become just like her. That's what hatred does."

I asked if I could get her another drink or some food, but she declined. She said,

"I'll sit here a while. It's peaceful."

I stood up, my sodden clothes itching my skin, asked,

"What will you do with Bill gone?"

"I'll tend his grave."

"If you ever need anything, you can get me at Bailey's Hotel."

"Thank you, Jack. Bill was lucky to have a friend like you."

When I got to the door of the pub, I looked back. She was watching the rain. Maybe it was a trick of the light, but she seemed content. I knew I wouldn't see her again. Opened the door, put my head down against the onslaught.

I was in my room in dry clothes, sitting on the bed, flicking through *Spirit Brides* by Kahlil Gibran.

After my encounter with Bill's sister, I wanted to be quiet, to read and to regroup. Don't know what possessed me to pick that book. Here's the piece I hit upon:

> *Woe unto this generation, for therein the verses of the Book have been reversed, the children eat unripe grapes and the father's teeth are set on edge. Go, Pious woman and pray for your insane son, that heaven might help him and return him to his senses.*

My mother would love that. I thought about what Fr Malachy had told me, about her stroke. The last thing in the world I wanted was to see her. Tossed and turned and eventually went to the window. The rain had stopped. I shook out my all-weather coat, decided to get it over with. Walked along Forster Street and stopped outside the site of the Magdalen. Soon, I'd go to call on Rita Monroe. What I'd tell her I had no idea. Would play it out as it happened.

Came to my mother's place, took a deep breath, knocked. The door was opened by a middle-aged woman in a nurse's uniform. She asked,

"Yes?"

"I'm Jack Taylor."

It took her a moment to process the information, then,

"The son?"

"Yes."

She seemed amazed. I said,

"Can I come in?"

"Oh . . . of course. I'm surprised."

As she stood aside to let me in, I asked,

"Why?"

"Fr Malachy mentioned you . . . but he said it was unlikely you'd come."

"He was wrong."

She led me into the kitchen, said,

"I'm Mrs Ross. I've only returned to nursing, to private nursing."

She'd just made tea, and a box of Jaffa cakes was open on the table. The radio was playing. Sinéad O'Connor had begun "Chiquitita".

We didn't speak till the song had finished. She said,

"I love Abba. I didn't think anyone else could do that song."

I wanted to say,

"You've tea, cakes and the radio. Where does the fucking nursing get a look in?"

But it was a little late to pull the concerned son gig. I asked,

"How is she?

The nurse threw a glance at the table, then folded her arms, said,

"I won't pretend it wasn't quite serious. However, she's made remarkable progress. The right side of her body and her face are paralysed and she hasn't recovered her speech. She is alert and getting stronger all the time."

I nodded, and she continued,

"Your mother is a saint. All the good work she's done in the parish. I've always admired her."

She stopped. This was my cue to row in with my part of the eulogy. I asked,

"Can I see her?"

I'd have been delighted if she refused, but she said,

"Of course. She's upstairs. I'll come with you."

"No need, you have your tea."

She didn't insist. I went up, paused a minute, knocked. Then realised she couldn't answer. I went in. If you had to put lines to my feeling then, you'd capture it with,

Mary, mother of celibate clerics who have turned their back on human love, would have presented Augustine with the perfect heavenly projection of his own domineering mother.

How the Irish Saved Civilization by Thomas Cahill.

I'd braced myself for her to look different. Hadn't braced enough. She was an old woman. The one characteristic she'd always had was energy. Sure, it was the dark kind, didn't spring from a source of goodness. Based more on a sense of grievance and a deep bitterness. Whatever else, it fuelled her so she'd always seemed in motion.

Seated in a chair, her whole body had diminished, as if she'd collapsed in on herself. The right arm was lying useless in her lap, her face was contorted, and a trace of spittle leaked from her lips. The hair, once a lustrous black, was completely white.

Worst of all, I didn't know how to address her. I stood near, said,

"Mother."

It sounded as stilted and awkward as that. I didn't so much sit on the bed as near collapse. I thought my mother had lost the ability to have such an effect on me. Her eyes had a dull sheen, seeing nothing. She didn't register my presence.

The silence was bewildering.

I'd never experienced her without the running mouth, usually littered with recriminations, vague threats, but definitely alive. I said,

"It's Jack."

And felt a tightness in my chest, added,

"Your son."

I'd tried to recall a time when I'd been close to her. Not a single incident surfaced. What I did remember was the constant belittlement of my father. He bore it without retaliation. As my passion for books grew, he had encouraged me. Built a large bookcase of which my mother was scornful.

"Books! You think they'll pay the rent."

I'd also discovered hurling. The two, books and sport, occupied every moment. My first day in Templemore, my mother had sold the books and burnt the bookcase. My father said,

"Your mother had a hard life."

Perhaps it was my first adult awareness. I'd answered,

"And she wants to make ours harder."

Now it was her turn. I moved to the sink, got a towel, brought it back. Carefully wiped the spit from her mouth, thought,

"What would it cost me to hug her?"

Couldn't do it.

When I'd been slung out of the guards, she said,

"I knew you'd come to nothing."

The worse I behaved, the better it suited her martyrdom. As I stared at her helplessness, I said,

"You'd think this would be the time for reconciliation, but what it is . . . is sad."

I moved to the door, was about to glance back, but she was

already burned into my soul. I walked down the stairs and the nurse appeared, asked,

"Did it go well?"

"Yes."

"I'm sure it was of great benefit to her."

I couldn't resist, asked,

"What makes you so sure?"

Flustered, she hesitated, then,

"I mean, knowing her son is here."

"She doesn't know shit."

The ferocity stunned us. I hadn't intended laying it off, but she was there. I looked at my right hand, so tight on the banister it seemed transparent. The nurse began to move towards the kitchen. I said,

"Call me if there's any change."

I'd gotten to the door when she said,

"I understand it's upsetting for you."

I wanted to turn, lash her understanding against the stairs, but settled for,

"Upsetting? Right, that's what it is."

I hope I didn't slam the door.

I walked down College Road, a sense of blackness dogging my footsteps. If I turned, I felt it would envelop me. The temptation to embrace the dark was compelling. The refrain from Death Row, "Dead Man Walking", played over and over in my ears. Alcoholics live on a daily basis with a sense of impending doom.

As I got to the Fair Green, a City Link coach was pulling out. An overpowering wish to be on it gripped me. I sat on the wall, all out of schemes, dreams and plans.

As close to total surrender as I've ever been.

In one of those inexplicable moments of serendipity, a

battered wino was sitting further down. He had a half dozen plastic bags spread round his feet. From one, he selected a bottle of Buckfast, put it on his head. I was as near to him as the length of a cigarette, looking right at him. He was oblivious to me or anyone else.

He began to sing, Abba again. I couldn't believe it.

"Fernando."

His voice was clear with a surety of style that was astonishing. I felt tears in my eyes and berated myself for crass sentimentality. Abba! . . . I mean . . . Come on.

"I'd write and I wouldn't lie. So when self-help writers tell one to find the child within, I assume they don't mean me."

Andrea Dworkin, *Heartbreak*

I got an early morning call from my solicitor. He began with,

"You paid the damages incurred to the chemist's window."

"I did."

"That has helped."

"Has it?"

"Oh, yes. I'm happy to inform you the other charges have been dropped."

"Even the guards?"

"I play golf with Clancy. A most accommodating chap. He certainly wouldn't want to pursue one of his own."

"He said that?"

"Not exactly, but you were a member of the force."

"I'm amazed."

"That's my job, amazing people."

"What can I say? Thank you."

"I'm not really the one to thank."

And he hung up.

I rang Kirsten. Took a while for her to answer then,

"Yes?"

"Kirsten, it's Jack."

A moment, then,

"You've had good news, I believe."

"Yes, I think you might have had some influence."

"You think?"

"Did you?"

"I'd hate to see you go to jail . . . or anybody else."

"Well, I appreciate it."

"See that you do."

Click.

The afternoon was bright, a suggestion of heat in the air. I walked to Newcastle. Time to face Rita Monroe. I wanted to see her reaction when I told her I knew who she was. Maybe she wouldn't even remember Bill's mother, but she would certainly remember the Magdalen, I'd make certain of that.

I rang her doorbell, my heart pounding. No answer. I stepped back to look up at the windows. A man came out of the adjoining house, said,

"You won't get an answer."

"Why not?"

"She's dead."

"What?"

"A heart attack, right there where you're standing. She'd been shopping; the groceries spilled all over the path."

"When?"

"Three days ago."

He examined me, said,

"You're not a relative?"

"No."

"Didn't think so. She kept herself to herself. Polite enough, but you couldn't call her friendly. Used to be a teacher, I hear."

I turned to go and he said,

"The house will be sold I expect."

Then added,

"Long as it isn't rented to students. Jeez, that would be just my luck."

For the next few weeks, I kept a low profile, cut way back on the pills and rationed myself to a few pints in the evening. Managed to steer clear of the whiskey. It was almost clean living, or as near as I could hope to get.

And I was reading, if not as fast as I could, at least as widely as I was able. Began to pay attention to the world again.

Jeffrey Archer went to jail, and dire predictions of recession were everywhere. Not that it was Archer's fault, but the two events coincided. Massive rioting in Genoa, and Tim Henman lost again at Wimbledon.

Mrs Bailey remarked,

"You seem to be leading a very quiet life."

I gave her the enigmatic smile to suggest it was part of a master plan, and she added,

"For a while there, the entire universe seemed to have fallen on you."

I was thinking a lot about evil and the various manifestations of it in my life. I didn't know if it was something in me that attracted it or if it was just random. I looked up Scott Peck for enlightenment. He said,

It is characteristic of those who are evil to judge others as evil. Unable to acknowledge their own imperfection, they must explain away their flaws by blaming others. And if necessary, they will even destroy others in the name of righteousness.

If you want to read hard solid cases of evil, then Peck's *People of the Lie* is hard to surpass.

Thought of the quiet life I was leading.

"I could get used to this."

Most evenings, I'd drop into Nestor's, shoot the breeze with Jeff. He said,

"The haunted look has left your eyes."

"I feel the freedom."

I even visited my mother a few times. There was no visible change in her condition, but there was a marked difference in my attitude. I didn't dread the visits and felt the wall of resentment begin to recede. I expected to hear from Terry Boyle, but no communication. What would I have told him? I'm not pursuing Kirsten because she saved me from jail?

The Department of Justice wrote their usual letter, demanding the return of the all-weather coat. As usual, I ignored them.

I was sitting in Nestor's, relishing the routine my life was becoming. A man came in, stood before me. It took me a few minutes to drag the face from my memory. He was young, with sallow skin. I ventured,

"Geraldo?"

I'd met him at the party; he was Terry's partner. He said,

"Yes . . . Terry said you always come here."

Even at the party, I'd felt there was something likable about him. I said,

"Can I get you a drink?"

"*Nada* . . . nothing . . . *gracias.*"

"Sit down."

He did.

He seemed to be on the brink of tears. I let him compose himself, asked,

"What's wrong?"

"Terry."

"Yes?"

"He is in a coma."

Pronounced it comma, continued,

"He went to see that woman."

Paused . . . moved to spit, said,

"That *diabla* . . . and now he's in the coma."

I didn't have to ask who the woman was, said,

"Kirsten. Tell me what happened."

"He went to her house. She says he had a drink . . . many drinks . . . maybe the drugs."

He looked beseechingly at me, cried,

"But Señor Taylor, you have been in his company. He takes one . . . two drinks . . . *todos* . . . no more . . . and the drugs, never. He hates them. She say he took many things. She go to bed, and in the morning, he is in the sickness."

I knew.

Jesus, she'd kept the liquid E, spiked his drink. My very words to her,

"You don't want to fuck with that stuff. It can cause a coma."

He began to sob. Jeff shot me an inquiring look, but I waved him off. I put my hand on Gerald's shoulder, said,

"I'll check it out, OK?"

Wiping his eyes, he said,

"*Gracias*. You think maybe he'll be all right?"

"Sure, sure he will."

He stood up, put out his hand. I said,

"Try not to worry, OK?"

When he'd gone, I thought about Terry and knew he sure as hell wasn't going to be all right

It didn't take me long to arrange the next step. I had most of
the ingredients already. Rang Ridge, said,

"If I wanted to be certain you'd respond to a burglary, how
would I arrange it?"

"What?"

"You heard me."

"What are you planning?"

"Ridge, you are going to respond to a break-in. In the course
of your investigation, you'll discover the solution to another
crime, a major crime. Should bump up your rating."

"I don't like the sound of this."

"You believe in justice or you just blowing smoke?"

Long silence, so I said,

"You'll have to trust me on this."

"That's the hard part."

I went for broke, added,

"Your uncle would have trusted me."

Deep sigh, then,

"I'd have to be in the operators' room when the call came
in."

"Tell me the time."

"Just after four this afternoon."

"OK, make sure you're there at that time. Now listen carefully: when you're at the house, be certain to look at the walk-
in closet in the bedroom. You'll see a pile of sweaters on a
shelf. Check them carefully. You got that, Nic an Iomaire?"

"You used my name."

"What?"

"Nic an Iomaire. You said it; you used the Irish form."

"Yeah, well, be sure you're there for the call."

I hung up.

Then I called Kirsten; she answered with an up-tempo
   "Hello!"
   "Kirsten, it's Jack."
   "How are you, Jack?"
   "Good. Listen, I need to see you."
   "Where and when, lover?"
   "Three forty-five in Jury's. Order some champagne; if I'm a
little late, start without me. I might be running a little behind."
   "What are we celebrating?"
   "It's a surprise."
   "I love surprises."
   "This is a whopper."
   Click.

I was outside her house at 3.30 p.m. A few minutes later a car
appeared, a BMW, Kirsten behind the wheel. She turned left,
drove down Taylor's Hill. I went up the drive and approached
the front door. Two hard kicks knocked it back and, pulling on
a pair of gloves, I went inside. Began to throw things around,
ransacking the rooms. Then upstairs and tossed the bedroom,
pulled open the walk-in closet. Took a deep breath, then scattered suits and shoes on the floor. The pile of sweaters was as
I remembered. I moved them around, then reached in my
pocket, took out Michael Neville's gun and the envelope with
his name and address, put them under the sweaters. Ensured
the end of the envelope was sticking out. Checked my watch:
3.45 p.m.
   I was in a phone kiosk at three minutes to four, rang the

guards, reported the burglary in progress and hung up. By 4.15 p.m., I was past Threadneedle Road and out on Salthill Prom-enade. The sight of the bay did what it always did.

Lifted my spirits.